Giovanni Francesco Pico

Giovanni Pico della Mirandola

His Life by his Nephew Giovanni Francesco Pico, also Three of his Letters,

his Interpretation of Psalm XVL

Giovanni Francesco Pico

Giovanni Pico della Mirandola
His Life by his Nephew Giovanni Francesco Pico, also Three of his Letters, his Interpretation of Psalm XVL

ISBN/EAN: 9783744696678

Printed in Europe, USA, Canada, Australia, Japan

Cover: Foto ©Raphael Reischuk / pixelio.de

More available books at **www.hansebooks.com**

GIOVANNI PICO DELLA MIRANDOLA.

₊ *Five hundred copies of this Edition are printed.*

GIOVANNI PICO DELLA MIRANDOLA:

HIS LIFE BY HIS NEPHEW GIOVANNI FRANCESCO PICO:

ALSO THREE OF HIS LETTERS; HIS INTERPRE-
TATION OF PSALM XVI.; HIS TWELVE RULES
OF A CHRISTIAN LIFE; HIS TWELVE
POINTS OF A PERFECT LOVER;
AND HIS DEPRECATORY
HYMN TO GOD.

TRANSLATED FROM THE LATIN BY
SIR THOMAS MORE.

EDITED WITH INTRODUCTION AND NOTES
By J. M. RIGG, ESQ.,
OF LINCOLN'S INN, BARRISTER-AT-LAW.

LONDON:
PUBLISHED BY DAVID NUTT IN THE STRAND.
MDCCCXC.

CHISWICK PRESS:—C. WHITTINGHAM AND CO., TOOKS COURT, CHANCERY LANE, LONDON.

INTRODUCTION.

IOVANNI PICO DELLA MIRAN-
DOLA, "the Phœnix of the wits," is
one of those writers whose personality
will always count for a great deal more
than their works. His extreme, almost
feminine beauty, high rank, and chival-.
rous character, his immense energy and versatility, his
insatiable thirst for knowledge, his passion for theorizing,
his rare combination of intellectual hardihood with genuine
devoutness of spirit, his extraordinary precocity, and his
premature death, make up a personality so engaging that
his name at any rate, and the record of his brief life,
must always excite the interest and enlist the sympathy
of mankind, though none but those, few in any genera-
tion, who love to loiter curiously in the bypaths of literature and philosophy, will ever care to follow his eager
spirit through the labyrinths of recondite speculation
which it once thridded with such high and generous hope.

For us, indeed, of the latter end of the nineteenth
century, trained in the exact methods, guided by the
steady light of modern philosophy and criticism, it is no
easy matter to enter sympathetically into the thoughts of

men who lived while as yet these were not, men who spent their strength in errant efforts, in blind gropings in the dark, on abortive half-solutions or no-solutions of problems too difficult for them, mere *ignes fatui*, it would seem, or at best mere brilliant meteor stars illuminating the intellectual firmament with a transitory trail of light, and then vanishing to leave the darkness more visible, yet without whose mistakes and failures and apparently futile waste of power philosophy and criticism would not have come into being.

Among such wandering meteoric apparitions not the least brilliant was Pico della Mirandola. Born in 1463, he grew to manhood in time to witness and participate in the effectual revival of Greek learning in Italy ; yet his earliest bias was scholastic, and a schoolman in grain he remained to the day of his death. How strongly he had felt the influence of the schoolmen, how little disposed he was to follow the humanistic hue and cry of indiscriminate condemnation, may be judged from the eloquent apology for them which, in the shape of a letter to his friend Ermolao Barbaro, he published in 1485. It was the fashion to stigmatize the schoolmen as barbarians because they knew no Greek and could not write classical Latin. That was the head and front of their offending in the eyes of men who had no idea of a better method of philosophizing than theirs, nor indeed any interest in philosophy, mere rhetoricians, grammarians, and pedagogues, while at any rate the schoolmen, however rude their style, were serious thinkers, who in grappling with the deepest problems of science human and divine displayed the rarest patience, sagacity, subtlety and ingenuity. Such is the gist of Pico's plea on behalf of the " barbarians," in urging which he exhausts the resources of rhetoric, and the ingenuity of

the advocate ; nor is there reason to doubt that it represents at least the embers of a very genuine enthusiasm.
That challenge, also, which he issued at Rome, and in
every university in Italy in the winter of 1486-7, summon-
ing as if by clarion call every intellectual knight-errant in
the peninsula to try conclusions with him in public dispu-
tation in the eternal city after the feast of Epiphany, does
it not recall the celebrated exploit of Duns Scotus at
Paris, when, according to the tradition, he won the title
of Doctor Subtilis by refuting two hundred objections to
the doctrine of the Immaculate Conception of the Virgin
Mary in a single day?   Only, as befitted " a great lord of
Italy," Pico's tournament is to be on a grander scale.
Duns had but one thesis to defend ; Pico offers to maintain nine hundred, and lest poverty should reduce the
number of his antagonists he offers to pay their travelling
expenses.   Moreover, to Duns, Aquinas, and other of the
schoolmen, Pico is beholden for not a few of his theses ;
of the rest, some are drawn direct from Plato, others from
Neo-Pythagorean, Neo-Platonic and syncretist writers,
while a certain number appear to be original.   Pico, however, was not so fortunate as Duns : the church smelt
heresy in his propositions, and Pope Innocent VIII.,
though he had at first authorised, was induced to pro-
hibit their discussion. (Bull dated 4th August, 1487).
Thirteen were selected for examination by a special
commission and were pronounced heretical.   Pico, however, so far from bowing to its decision, wrote in hot
haste an elaborate " Apologia " or defence of his orthodoxy, which, had it not been more ingenious than
conclusive, might perhaps have been accepted ; as it was,
it only brought him into further trouble.

This Apology " elucubrated," as he tells, " properante

stilo" in twenty nights, Pico dedicated to Lorenzo de' Medici, modestly describing it as "exiguum sane munus, sed fidei meae, sed observantiae profecto in omne tempus erga te maxime non leve testimonium," "a trifling gift indeed, but as far as possible from being a slight token of my loyalty, nay, of my devotion to you." Hasty though its composition was, it certainly displays no lack of either ingenuity, subtlety, acuteness, learning, or style. Evidently written out of a full mind, it represents Pico's mature judgment upon the abstruse topics which it handles, and is a veritable masterpiece of scholastic argumentation. After a brief prologue detailing the circumstances which gave occasion to the work Pico proceeds to discuss *seriatim* the thirteen "damnatæ conclusiones," and the several objections which had been made to them. The tone throughout is severe and dry and singularly free from heat or asperity. Some of the theses are treated at considerable length, others dismissed in a page or two, or even less. Altogether, when the rapidity of its composition is borne in mind, the treatise appears little less a prodigy.

The obnoxious theses were as follows :—(1) That Christ did not truly and in real presence, but only *quoad effectum*, descend into hell; (2) that a mortal sin of finite duration is not deserving of eternal but only of temporal punishment; (3) that neither the cross of Christ, nor any image, ought to be adored in the way of worship; (4) that God cannot assume a nature of any kind whatsoever, but only a rational nature; (5) that no science affords a better assurance of the divinity of Christ than magical and cabalistic science; (6) that assuming the truth of the ordinary doctrine that God can take upon himself the nature of any creature whatsoever, it is possible for the body of Christ to be present on the altar without the conversion of the substance of the bread or the annihilation of " paneity ;" (7) that it is more rational to believe that Origen is saved than that he is damned ; (8) that as no one's opinions are just such as he wills them to be, so no one's beliefs are just such as he wills them to be ; (9) that the inseparability of subject and accident may be maintained consistently with the doctrine of transubstantiation ; (10) that the words "hoc est corpus" pronounced during the consecration of the bread are to be taken " materialiter" (i.e., as a mere recital) and not "significative" (i.e., as denoting an actual fact); (11) that the miracles of Christ are a most certain proof of his divinity, by reason not of the works themselves, but of his manner of doing them ; (12) that it is more improper to say of God that he is intelligent, or intellect, than of an angel that it is a rational soul; (13) that the soul knows nothing in act and distinctly but itself.

It is undeniable that some of these propositions smack somewhat rankly of heresy, and Pico's ingenuity is taxed to the uttermost to give them even a semblance of congruity with the doctrines of the Church. The following, however, is the gist of his defence. Christ, he argues, did actually descend into hell, but only in spirit, not in bodily presence ; eternal punishment is inflicted on the finally impenitent sinner not for his sins done in the flesh, which are finite, but for his impenitence, which is necessarily infinite ; the cross is to be adored, but only as a symbol, not in and for itself, for which he cites Scotus, admitting that St. Thomas is against him. The thesis that God cannot take upon himself a nature of any kind whatsoever, but only a rational nature, must be understood without prejudice to the omnipotence of God, which is not in question ; God cannot assume the nature of any irrational creature, because by the very act of so doing he necessarily raises it to himself, endows it with a rational nature. The thesis that no science gives us better assurance of the divinity of Christ than magical and cabalistic science referred to such sciences only as do not rest on revelation, and among them to the science of natural magic, which treats of the virtues and activities of natural agents and their relations *inter se*, and that branch only of cabalistic science which is concerned with the virtues of celestial bodies ; which of all natural sciences furnish the most convincing proof of the divinity of Christ, because they show that his miracles could not have been performed by natural agencies. The sixth thesis must not be understood as if Pico maintained that the bread was not converted into the body of Christ, but only that it is possible that the bread and the body may be mysteriously linked together without the one being converted into the other, which would be quite consistent with the words of St. Paul, 1 Cor. x. 16 : " The bread which we break is it not the communion of the body of Christ ? " if interpreted figuratively. With regard to the salvation of Origen, Pico plunges with evident zest into the old controversy as to the authenticity of the heretical passages in that writer's works, and urges that his damnation can at most be no more than a pious opinion. In justification of the position that belief is not a mere matter of will he cites the authority of Aristotle and St. Augustine, adding a brief summary of the evidences of the Christian faith, to wit, prophecy, the harmony of the Scriptures, the authority of their authors, the reasonableness of their contents, the unreasonableness of their contents, the unreasonableness of particular heresies, the stability of the Church, the miracles. As to transubstantiation, Pico professes himself to hold the doctrine of the Church, merely adding thereto the pious opinion that the Thomist distinction between real existence and essence is consistent with the theory that the bread itself remains in spite of the transmutation of its substance, and thus with the doctrine of the inseparability of subject and accident ; as for the words " hoc est corpus," it appears from their context and their place in the office that they are not to be taken literally, for the priest, when in consecrating the bread he says, " Take, eat," does not suit the action to the word by offering the bread to the communicants, but takes it himself, and so when in consecrating the wine he says, "qui pro vobis et pro multis effundetur," it is not to be supposed, as if the words were to be taken literally it must be supposed, that he means that the blood of Christ actually will be shed, or that he does not mean to claim the benefit of it for himself as well as the congregation, and the "many." That the value of Christ's miracles as evidences of his divinity lies rather in the way in which they were wrought than in the works themselves, is supported by Christ's own words in St. John xiv. 12 : " Verily, verily, I say unto you, He that believeth on me, the works that I do shall he do also ; and greater works than these shall he do ; because I go to my Father ; " which are quite inconsistent with the idea that the works are themselves evidence of his divinity. In support of the proposition that intellect or intelligence cannot properly be ascribed to God, Pico invokes the authority of Dionysius the Areopagite, who holds the same doctrine, but does not on that account deny to God an altogether superior faculty of cognition, even farther removed from angelic intelligence than that is from human reason. The last proposition, viz., that the soul knows nothing in act and distinctly but itself, being extremely subtle and profound, Pico forbears to enlarge upon it, pointing out, however, that it has the authority of St. Augustine in its favour. The reference is to the De Trinitate, x. 14.[1] The doctrine itself is of peculiar interest, for in it lay the germ of the Cartesian philosophy.

Pico concludes the "Apologia" with an eloquent appeal to his critics to judge him fairly, which was so little heeded that some of them saw fit to impugn its good faith, and raised such a clamour about it that Pico, who in the meantime had gone to France, was peremptorily recalled to Rome by the Pope. He complied, but through the influence of Lorenzo was permitted to reside in the Benedictine monastery at Fiesole, while the new charge was under investigation. Meanwhile Garsias, Bishop of Ussel, published (1489) an elaborate examination of the " Apologia," nor did Pico hear the last of the affair until shortly before his death, when Alexander VI., by a Bull dated 18th June, 1493, acquitted him of heresy and assured him of immunity from further annoyance.

An oration on man and his place in nature—with which Pico had designed to introduce his theses to the

[1] Utrum emin aeris sit vis vivendi, reminiscendi, volendi, cogitandi, sciendi, judicandi ; an ignis, an cerebri, an sanguinis, an atomorum, an præter usitata quatuor elementa quinti nescio cujus corporis, an ipsius carnis nostræ compago vel temperamentum hæc efficere valeat, dubitaverunt homines : et alius hoc, alius aliud affirmare conatus est. Vivere se tamen et meminisse, et intelligere, et velle, et cogitare, et scire, et judicare quis dubitet ? Quandoquidem etiam si dubitat, vivit : si dubitat unde dubitet, meminit ; si dubitat, dubitare se intelligit ; si dubitat, certus esse vult ; si dubitat, cogitat ; si dubitat, scit se nescire ; si dubitat, judicat non se temere consentire oportere. Quisquis igitur aliunde dubitat, de his omnibus dubitare non debet : quæ si non essent de ulla re dubitare non posset.

learned audience which he had hoped to gather about him to listen to the discussion—was not published until after his death. The theme is the familiar one of the dignity of man as the only terrestrial creature endowed with free will, and thus capable of developing into an angel and even becoming one with God, or declining into a brute or even a vegetable. On this Pico descants at some length and with much eloquence, and a great display of erudition—Schoolman and Neo-Platonist, Cabalist and Pythagorean, Moses and Plato, Job, Seneca, Cicero, and the Peripatetics jostling one another in his pages in the most *bizarre* fashion. With Pico, as with Dante, theology is the queen of the sciences, and the true end of man is so to purify the soul by the practice of virtue and the study of philosophy — moral and natural—as that it may be capable of the knowledge and the love of God. His own theological speculations are contained in three works, viz.: (1) a commentary on the first twenty-six verses of the first chapter of Genesis, published in 1489, under the title of "Heptaplus," and dedicated to Lorenzo de' Medici; (2) an essay towards the reconcilation of Plato and Aristotle, entitled "De Ente et Uno," published in 1491; (3) a commentary on Girolamo Benivieni's "Canzone dello Amore Celeste e Divino," the date of which has not been precisely fixed.

This curious trilogy is a signal example of the insane extravagances into which an acute and subtle intellect may be led by philosophical and theological *arrière pensée*. Pico's problem is essentially the same with that on which the most powerful and ingenious minds of the Middle Ages had spent their strength in vain, to wit—how to reconcile theology and philosophy. The difference is that, whereas the older thinkers had but little knowledge of any other philosopher than Aristotle, and knew him but imperfectly, Pico in the full tide of the renaissance has to grapple with the gigantic task of reconciling Catholic doctrine not merely with Aristotle, but with Plato, the Neo-Platonists, Neo-Pythagoreans, the pseudo-Dionysius the Areopagite, the Orphic and Hermetic theosophies, and indeed with whatever of recondite, obscure, and mysterious in that kind the Pagan world had given birth to. The result is what might be expected — the wildest possible jumble of incompatible ideas, which not even the most dexterous legerdemain can twist into the remotest semblance of congruity.

In the dedicatory letter prefixed to the " Heptaplus " Pico explains to Lorenzo the scheme of the work, and the motives which induced him to undertake it. Besides the inestimable advantage which he derived from being the immediate recipient of divine revelation, Moses, it appears, was the greatest of all philosophers. Was he not versed in all the science of the Egyptians, and was not Egypt the source whence the Greeks drew their inspiration ? Was not Plato rightly called by Numenius[1] Μωσῆς Ἀττικίζων ? True it is that Moses has not the least of the appearance of a philosopher, but even in the account of the creation seems only to be telling a very plain and simple story, but that must not be allowed to detract from his claims. Doubtless he veiled a profound meaning under this superficial show of simplicity, and spoke in enigmas, or allegories, even as Plato and Jesus Christ were wont to do, in order that they might not be

---

[1] Numenius of Apameia in Syria, a syncretistic philosopher, supposed to have lived in the age of the Antonines. For the phrase see Mullach, *Frag. Phil. Græc.* iii. 167.

understood except by those to whom it was given to understand mysteries.

In all true wisdom there should be an element of mystery; it would not be right that everyone should be able to understand it. The task of interpreting the Mosaic account of the creation has been taken in hand by a host of writers, who have struggled mightily with three cardinal difficulties, which, it would seem, they have one and all failed to surmount. These difficulties are (1) to avoid attributing to Moses commonplace or inadequate ideas; (2) to make the interpretation consecutive and consistent from beginning to end; (3) to bring him into harmony with subsequent thinkers. Where his predecessors have failed Pico hopes to succeed.

The interpretation is worthy of the proem. In the threefold division of the Tabernacle Pico finds a type of the three spheres—angelic or intelligible, celestial, and sublunary—which, with man, the microcosm, make up the universe; and thus has no difficulty in understanding why the veil of the Temple was rent when Christ opened a way for man into the super-celestial sphere. These four worlds are all one, not only because all have the same first principle and the same final cause, and are linked together by certain general harmonies and affinities, but also because whatever is found in the sublunary sphere has its counterpart in the other two, but of a nobler character (*meliore nota*). Thus to terrestrial fire corresponds in the celestial sphere the sun; in the super-celestial, seraphic intelligence. Similarly, what is water on earth is in the heavens the moon, and in the super-celestial region cherubic intelligence. "The elementary fire burns, the celestial vivifies, the super-celestial loves." What cherubic intelligence does Pico forgets to say; but fire and water being opposed, it is clear that it ought to hate.

In the intelligible world God, surrounded by nine orders of angels, unmoved Himself, draws all to Himself; to whom in the celestial world corresponds the stable empyrean with its nine revolving spheres; in the sublunary world the first matter with its three elementary forms, earth, water, and fire, the three orders of vegetable life, herbs, plants, and trees, and the three sorts of "sensual souls," zoophytic, brutish, human, making together "nine spheres of corruptible forms."

Man, the microcosm, unites all three spheres; having a body mixed of the elements, a vegetal soul, and the senses of the brute, reason or spirit, which holds of the celestial sphere, and an angelic intellect, in virtue of which he is the very image of God.

Now it is true that Moses in his account of the creation appears to ignore all this, but it is not for us on that account to impute to him ignorance of it. On the contrary, we must suppose that his cosmogony is equally true of each of the four worlds which make up the universe, and must accordingly give it a fourfold interpretation. A fifth chapter will be rendered necessary by the difference between the four worlds, and a sixth by their affinities and community.

We have thus six chapters corresponding with the six days of creation. A seventh is devoted to expounding the meaning of the Sabbath rest; and to indicate this sevenfold division of the work Pico entitles it "Heptaplus."

The plural method of interpreting Scripture, it must be observed, was by no means peculiar to Pico, indeed was in common use in his day. As a rule, however, commentators were content with three senses, which they distinguished as mystical, anagogical, and allegorical. To

Pico's philosophic mind this, no doubt, seemed a pitiful empiricism. For what was the ground of the triple method? Why these three senses and no more? He scorned such grovelling economy and rule of thumb, and determined to place the interpretation of the Mosaic cosmogony once for all on a firm and philosophic basis. Digging, accordingly, deep into the nature of things for the root, as he calls it, of his exegesis, he comes upon the Ptolemaic system with its central earth surrounded by its nine concentric revolving spheres, the nearest that of the moon, the most remote that of the fixed stars, in the interspace the solar and other planetary spheres, and beyond all the stable empyrean. To this he joins the Platonic theory of an intelligible world behind the phenomenal, and the Christian idea of heaven, borrows from the pseudo-Dionysius the Areopagite his nine orders of angels to correspond with the nine celestial spheres, discerns in the stable empyrean the type of the immutability of God, in matter as the promise and potency of all things, the evidence of His infinite power and fulness, throws in the Neo-Platonic doctrine of the microcosm and macrocosm, and lo! the work is done, and a cosmology constructed, which to elicit from Genesis may well demand a sevenfold method of interpretation. The minor details of this curious mosaic, to wit, the correspondence between the nine spheres of corruptible forms and the nine planets, between seraphic intelligence and the sun, between cherubic intelligence and the moon, seem, for what they are worth, to be all Pico's own.

Having thus found, as he thinks, a philosophic basis for his exegetical method, Pico proceeds to apply it to the Mosaic text with the utmost rigour and vigour. It would be tedious to follow him through all the minutiæ of his elaborate and extraordinary interpretation. A few examples of his art will amply suffice; and we cannot do better than begin at the beginning. What, then, did Moses mean by "In the beginning"? The solution of this weighty problem Pico plainly regards as his greatest triumph, and accordingly reserves it for the closing chapter, when he introduces it with a mighty flourish of trumpets. These pregnant words, "In the beginning," contain, it appears, the following mystic sentence: "Pater in Filio et per Filium, principium et finem, sive quietem, creavit caput, ignem, et fundamentum magni hominis fœdere bono," which is elicited from them by various dexterous permutations and combinations of the letters which make up their Hebrew equivalent. The key to the interpretation of the sentence is found in the idea of the microcosm.

Man being the microcosm, the macrocosm, or universe, may be called "magnus homo," whose "caput," or head, is the supercelestial or intelligible world, while his "ignis," fire, or heart, is the celestial world or empyrean, and his "fundamentum," or base, the sublunary sphere, all which are bound together "fœdere bono," by ties of kinship and congruity. In plain English, then, the initial words of the first chapter of Genesis mean, according to Pico :—"The Father in the Son, and by the Son, who is the beginning and the end, or rest, created the head, the heart, and the lower parts of the great man fitly joined together;" and thus contain an implicit prophecy of the Christian dispensation.

After this splendid *tour de force*, everything else in Pico's exposition will seem tame and trivial. We may observe, however, that four being a square number, he finds in the fourth day an adumbration of the fulness of time in which Christ came to earth; in the sun, moon, and stars types of

Christ, His Church, and His Apostles; in the waters under the firmament, which on the third day were gathered together unto one place, a type of the Gentiles; in the earth, a type of the Israelites; and in the fact that before the creation of the sun the waters produced nothing, and the earth little that was good, while after the sun had shone upon them they became fruitful abundantly of moving creatures, birds, and fishes, a prophecy of the spiritual revolution wrought by Christianity—were not the Apostles fishers of men? and a plain, unmistakable proof that his exposition is no mere fancy, but solid truth. It is absurd to criticize such folly seriously, but it may be worth while to note in passing that Christ being according to Christian theology co-eternal with the Father, the creation of the sun serves but ill as a type of His advent.

Pico, however, is so little disturbed by this consideration, that he finds another type of Christ in another created object — to wit, the firmament — which, while separating the waters above it from those below, nevertheless unites them as every mean unites its extremes, and thus enables the former to fecundate the latter, as Christ enables the divine grace to descend upon man. At the same time, however, he is careful to affirm the orthodox position that Christ is the first begotten of every creature.

Such are some of the meanings which Pico finds in the Mosaic text when interpreting it of the creation of the intelligible or super-celestial sphere. The same terms have, of course, quite different imports when applied to the creation of the other spheres. Thus, in relation to the sublunary sphere, " heaven" means efficient cause, " the earth" matter, and " the waters" on the face of which the Spirit of God moved, the accidents of matter.

But the reader has probably had already far too much of these absurdities, which, however, when due allowance has been made for the differences of the times, are perhaps hardly grosser than some of the ingenious attempts by which more recent writers have sought to reconcile Genesis with modern science.

It is time, however, to take a glance at the treatise "De Ente et Uno." This little tractate purports to be an essay towards the reconciliation of Plato and Aristotle —an essentially hopeless undertaking, on which Poryhyry had long before spent his strength for nought. We may therefore spare ourselves the trouble of even asking how far Pico is successful. The interest of the treatise consists in the insight which it affords into Pico's own views of the nature of God and His relation to the world. It is, in fact, a chapter, and by no means an unimportant chapter, in the long dialectic on the nature of universals and their relation to particulars, which formed the staple of mediæval thought. All cultivated people have heard of this great debate, but few have any clear idea of the issues involved in it, and why so many subtle and ingenious thinkers spent their best energies upon it. Nay, it is sometimes contemptuously dismissed by those who should know better as mere piece of frivolous logomachy. In truth, however, this apparently barren controversy was big with the most momentous of all the problems with which the human mind can concern itself—first, "Utrum sit Deus"—whether God exist? second, if He exist, in what way His relation to the universe is to be understood—whether in the way of a transcendent cause or an immanent principle, or in both ways at once?

Saturated as mediæval theology was with ideas derived from Plato and Aristotle, and but imperfectly understood, it was inevitable that when men attempted to philosophize about God, they should conceive Him—or at any rate tend to conceive Him—rather as a universal principle, or archetypal source of ideas, than as a concrete personality. Hence nominalism, with its frank denial of the existence of universals, conceptualism with its reduction of them to figments of abstraction, seemed equally to involve atheism; even realism of the more moderate type, which, while asserting the objective existence of the universal, denied its existence *ante rem*—*i.e.*, apart from the particular—was viewed with suspicion as tending to merge God in the cosmos; while realism of the high Platonic order, by its assertion of the existence of a world of pure universals—archetypes of the particulars revealed to sense—found favour in the eyes of men in whom the philosophic interest was always strictly subordinated to the theological.

In the treatise " De Ente et Uno " the question as between the transcendence and the immanence of God comes to the surface with remarkable abruptness. Is "the One," *i.e.* God, to be regarded as " Being " or as " above Being ? " Aristotle is supposed to maintain the former position, Plato undoubtedly holds the latter. To the Platonic doctrine Pico gives in his unqualified adhesion, and attempts to constrain Aristotle to do so likewise. His Platonism is of the most uncompromising type, the idealism of the Parmenides with the Parmenidean doubts and difficulties left out. Abstract terms such as " whiteness " or " humanity " signify, he asserts dogmatically, and apparently without a shadow of doubt as to the truth of the doctrine, real existences which are what they are in their own right

xxi

and not by derivation from or participation in anything else, while their corresponding concretes denote existences of an inferior order which are what they are by virtue of their participation in the abstract or archetypal ideas. Upon this theory he proceeds deliberately to base his theology. As whiteness in itself is not white, but the archetypal cause of that particular appearance in objects, and in the same way heat in itself is not hot, but the cause of the particular sensation which we call heat; so God is not " Being" though, or rather because, He is the "fulness," *i.e.* the archetypal cause, of " Being." As thus the one primal fountain of " Being " He is properly described as " the One." " God is all things and most eminently and most perfectly all things ; which cannot be, unless He so comprehends the perfections of all things in Himself as to exclude whatever imperfection is in them. Now, things are imperfect either (1) in virtue of some defect in themselves, whereby they fall short of the normal standard proper to them, or (2) in virtue of the very limitations which constitute them particular objects. It follows that God being perfect has in Him neither any defect nor any particularity, but is the abstract universal unity of all things in their perfection. It is, therefore, not correct to say that He comprehends all things in Himself; for in that case neither would He be perfectly simple in nature, nor would they be infinite which are in Him, but He would be an infinite unity composed of many things infinite, indeed, in number, but finite in respect of perfection ; which to speak or think of God is profanity." In other words, in order to get a true idea of God we must abstract from all plurality, all particularity whatever, and then we have as the residue the notion of a most perfect, infinite, perfectly simple being. God may, then, be called Being itself, the One itself, the Good itself, the True itself; but it is better to describe Him as that which is "above Being, above truth, above unity, above goodness, since His Being is truth itself, unity itself, goodness itself," better still to say of Him that He is "intelligibly and ineffably above all that we can most perfectly say or conceive of Him," and with Dionysius the Areopagite to define him by negatives. And so he quotes with approval part of the closing sentence of the treatise "De Mystica Theologia" in which agnosticism seems to exhaust itself in the exuberant detail of its negations. "It" (*i.e.* the First Cause) "is neither truth, nor dominion, nor wisdom, nor the One, nor unity, nor Deity, nor goodness, nor spirit, as far as we can know; nor sonship nor fatherhood, nor aught else of things known to us or any other creature; neither is it aught of things that are not nor of things that are; nor is it known to any as it is itself nor knows them itself as they are; whose is neither speech, nor name, nor knowledge, nor darkness, nor light, nor error, nor truth, nor any affirmation or negation." And then, to give a colour of orthodoxy to his doctrine he quotes the authority of St. Augustine to the effect that "the wisdom of God is no more wisdom than justice, His justice no more justice than wisdom, His life no more life than cognition, His cognition no more cognition than life; for all these qualities are united in God not in the way of confusion or combination or by the interpenetration as it were of things in themselves distinct, but by way of a perfectly simple ineffable fontal unity": a summary statement of some passages in the sixth book of the treatise "De Trinitate," which is of course misleading apart from the context in which they occur.

Such is Pico's theory of the Godhead—a theory which

in fact reduces it to the mere abstraction of perfect simplicity and universality, a theory wholly irreconcilable with the Christian faith, wholly unfit to form the basis of religion. Nor was its author insensible, rather he would seem to have been only too painfully conscious of the barrenness of the results to which so much toil and trouble had brought him; for he has no sooner enunciated it than he turns, as if with a sigh, to Politian, and addresses him thus :—" But see, my Angelo, what madness possesses us. Love God while we are in the body we rather may than either define or know Him. By loving Him we more profit ourselves, have less trouble, please Him better. Yet had we rather ever seeking Him by the way of speculation never find Him than by loving Him possess that which without loving were in vain found "—words that since Pico's day must have found an echo in the heart of many a thinker weary with the vain effort to gain by philosophical methods a clear insight into the divine nature.

The treatise involved Pico in an amicable controversy with his friend Antonio da Faenza (Antonius Faventinus or Cittadinus), who criticised it in some detail, and to whom Pico replied with no less detail. The correspondence was protracted during his life, and was continued after his death by his nephew, but it sheds little additional light on Pico's views. How far he seriously held them, and whether he had some esoteric method of reconciling them with the orthodox faith, are questions which we have no means of answering. It is curious, however, in reference to this matter, to compare the opening chapters of his commentary on Girolamo Benivieni's *canzone* on "Celestial Love." Benivieni also was a Platonist, and having saturated himself with the Symposium and the Phædrus, the fifth book of the third Ennead of Plotinus, and Ficino's commentaries, thought himself qualified to write a *canzone* on ideal love which should put Guinicelli and Cavalcanti to shame. The result was that he produced a *canzone* which has a certain undeniable elevation of style, but is so obscure that even with the help of Pico's detailed commentary it takes some hard study to elicit its meaning. The theme, however, is the purifying influence of love in raising the soul through various stages of refinement from the preoccupation with sensuous beauty to the contemplation of the ideal type of the beautiful, and thence to the knowledge of God, who, though, as Pico is careful to explain, He is not beautiful Himself, since beauty implies an element of variety repugnant to His nature, is nevertheless the source of the beautiful no less than of the true and the good.

The commentary consists of two parts; the first a philosophical dissertation on love in general, its nature, origin, and place in the universal scheme of things; the second a detailed analysis and exposition of the poem, stanza by stanza, almost line by line. Both parts, in spite of the good Italian in which they are written, are unspeakably tedious, being mostly made up of bald rationalizations of Greek myths. The first few chapters, however, are theological or theosophical; and here we find God described consistently with the doctrine of the " De Ente et Uno " as "ineffably elevated above all intellect and cognition," while beneath Him, and between the intelligible and the sensible worlds is placed " a creature of nature as perfect as it is possible for a creature to be," whom God creates from eternity, whom alone He immediately creates, and who " by Plato and likewise by the ancient philosophers, Mercury Trismegistus and

Zoroaster is called now the Son of God, now Mind, now Wisdom, now Divine Reason." Here we have a fusion and confusion of the "self-sufficing and most perfect God" created by the Demiurge of Plato's Timæus to be the archetype of the world, the Son of God of Philo and later theosophists, and the Νοῦς of Plotinus, the first emanation of the Godhead. This Son of God, however, Pico bids us observe, is not to be confounded with the Son of God of Christian theology, who is Creator and not creature, but may be regarded as "the first and most noble angel created by God."

This is virtually Pico's last word on theology or theosophy, and it leaves the question of his orthodoxy an insoluble enigma. Did he really believe in the Son of God of Christian theology, or had he not rather dethroned Him in favour of the syncretistic abstraction which he calls the first and most noble angel created by God, though he was too timid to avow the fact. We have seen that he did not scruple to find types of Christ in created things, such as the firmament and the sun. Little stress can be laid on this, and if it stood alone it might be dismissed as a piece of sheer inadvertence, but read in connection with the pregnant passage from the commentary on Benivieni's poem, it certainly makes in favour of the idea that in the passion for unity which evidently possessed him Pico had abandoned his trinitarianism, and that the treatise "De Ente et Uno" contains his most mature and profound theological convictions. If so, the caution against confusing the two Sons of God must be interpreted as a mere device to save appearances.

However this may be, it is undeniable that Pico was, even in the conventional Christian sense, a sincerely religious man. The letter to his nephew, Giovanni

Francesco, on the spiritual life, translated by More, has in it the ring of genuine simple Christian godliness, and though Savonarola saw fit to consign him to the purgatorial fire for his refusal to devote himself entirely to the religious life, he did so probably rather in sorrow than in anger, on the principle that whom the Lord loveth He chasteneth, regarding Pico as one who had in him the making of a saint, but who by a *gran rifiuto* failed of attaining unto the prize of his high calling.

That Pico should have found a theology which reduces God to a *caput mortuum* of which nothing can be said but that it is above all things, and Christ to a "great angel," the first of created beings, compatible with the simple and ardent piety of a Catholic saint would indeed be a notable phenomenon, but, at the same time, one which sound criticism would accept without attempting to account for it, much less to explain it away. No exercise of ingenuity would ever succeed in harmonising his theology with the Catholic or any form of the Christian faith, and it is equally impossible to dispute the sincerity of his piety. It is all part and parcel of the peculiar, unique idiosyncracy of the man's nature, a nature compounded of mysticism and rationalism, credulity and scepticism, in about equal proportions.

He finds strange hidden meanings in the simple words of Moses, he believes in natural magic, and holds that it testifies more clearly of Christ than any other science, yet he cannot credit the story of Christ's descent into hell, or the doctrine of transubstantiation, or the eternity of punishment, and writes an elaborate treatise in twelve books against the pretensions of astrology. A man of immense and varied learning, not merely classical but oriental, he yet permitted himself to be imposed on by a

Sicilian Jew, to whom he gave an immense sum for some worthless cabalistic treatises, under the impression that they were the lost works of Ezra.

Perhaps it is unfair to take seriously what may have been merely a compliment less sincere than gracious ; but it certainly does not tend to raise one's impression of his critical powers to find Pico, in a letter to Lorenzo de' Medici, setting Lorenzo's insipid verses above anything that Dante or Petrarch ever wrote.

With all this it is more easy to do injustice than justice to Pico. It is impossible to study him attentively without seeing at last that amidst all his vagaries, absurdities, perversities, there was real faculty in him, and faculty of an order which, matured by a severer discipline than his age could afford, would have won for him a place, though perhaps no very exalted one, among philosophers. The philosophic instinct, without doubt, he had, and in high measure, a veritable passion not merely for truth but for a consistent, harmonious body of truth. The high originative faculty which discovers a method was denied him. Hence he remained a mere syncretist forlornly struggling to weave the discordant utterances of rival schools into a coherent system. His importance for the student of philosophy is that he made this attempt, made it with wider knowledge and more passionate zeal than any of his predecessors, and failed, and that with his failure scholasticism as a movement came to an end. Individual thinkers indeed there have been, such as Leibniz and Coleridge, in whom something of Pico's spirit has survived, whose laudable anxiety to justify the ways of God to man has led them to attempt the reconciliation of the irreconcilable, of atomism, *e.g.*, with idealism, of transcendentalism with the Christian faith, and such men are in effect schoolmen born out of due time. Nevertheless that which in the specific sense we call scholasticism made in Pico its final effort, was beaten by the sheer intractability of its problem, which the new learning made ever more apparent, and died out.

Schoolman, however, though Pico was, it must not be forgotten that he was also a humanist. His style, even where, as in the "Apologia," he is at his driest and most formal, and in the attempt to reconcile his heresies with Catholic doctrine, becomes, in the fineness of his distinctions, almost more scholastic than the subtlest doctor that ever spun intellectual cobwebs in Oxford or Paris, effectually distinguishes him from "the barbarians," and proclaims him a child of the renaissance ; and long and justly celebrated were the "golden letters" in which, in all the luxuriance of Ciceronic periods, he praises Politian's translation of the *Enchiridion* of Epictetus or Lorenzo's verses, discusses the rival claims of the old and new learning with Ermolao Barbaro, descants on the regal dignity of philosophy and philosophers to Andrea Corneo, exhorts his nephew to the practice of the Christian life, or expatiates to Ficino on his new-born zeal for oriental studies.

In none of these does he appear to better advantage than in one of the earliest, written in reply to a flattering letter from Politian, which in effect admitted him to the confraternity of learned men.

"I am as much beholden to you," he writes, "for the high praise you give me in your last letter as I am far from deserving it. For one is beholden to another for what he gives, not for what he pays. Wherefore, indeed, I am beholden to you for all that you write of me, since in me there is nothing of the kind, for you in no way owed it to

me, but it all came of your courtesy and singular gracious-
ness towards me. For the rest, if you examine me, you
will find nothing in me that is not slight, humble, strictly
limited. I am a novice, a tiro, and have advanced but a
step, no more, from the darkness of ignorance. It is a compliment to place me in the rank of a student. Something
more is meant by a man of learning, a title appropriate
only to you and your likes, too grand for me; since of
those matters which in letters are most important I have
as yet obtained no thorough knowledge, scarcely more
indeed than, as it were, a peep through a lattice window. I
will endeavour indeed, and that I now do, to become some
time or another such as you say and either really think,
or at any rate would fain think, that I am. Meantime I
will follow your example, Angelo, who excuse yourself to
the Greeks by the fact that you are a Latin, to the Latins
on the ground that you grecize. I too will have recourse to
a similar subterfuge, and claim the indulgence of the poets
and rhetoricians because I am said to philosophize, of the
philosophers because I play the rhetorician and cultivate
the Muses; though my case is very different from yours.
For in sooth while I desire to sit, as they say, on two
chairs, I fall between them, and it turns out at last (to be
brief) that I am neither a poet, nor a rhetorician, nor a
philosopher." How strictly these gloomy forebodings
were realised in the matter of philosophy we have already
seen. From attempting to decide how far his cultivation
of the Muses was rewarded we are precluded by Pico's
own act, the destruction of his early love poems. Of these
the following sonnet alone has been preserved :—

Da poi che i duo belli occhi che mi fanno
    Cantar del mio Signor sì nuovamente,
    Avvamparo la mia gelata mente,
    Già volge in lieta sorte il second' anno.

Felice giorno, ch'a sì dolce affanno
  Fu bel principio ; onde nel cor si sente
  Una fiamma girar sì dolcemente,
  Che men beati son que' che 'n ciel stanno.

L'ombra, il pensier, la negligenza, e'l letto
  M'avean ridotto, ove la maggior parte
  Giace ad ogn' or del vulgo errante e vile.

Scorsemi Amore a più gradito oggetto :
  E se cosa di grato oggi a 'l mio stile,
  Madonna affina in me l'ingegno e l'arte.

Since first the light of those twin stars, thine eyes,
  That me to hymn my Lord thus newly move,
  Kindled my frost-bound soul with fires of love,
  Years twain their course have run in happy wise.

O blessed day, of such sweet heaviness
  Such fair beginning !   Since when to and fro
  Within my heart a gentle flame doth go,
  That not in heaven is found such happiness.

Recluse I lived, in musing lost, nor care,
  Nor action knew, wellnigh become a part
  Of the vile herd of errant men and base.

Love roused my soul to seek an end more fair :
  And if my style to-day has aught of grace
  My lady 'tis refines my mind and art.

If this somewhat insipid sonnet is a fair sample of Pico's amatory effusions, one can more readily understand why he burned them than the regret which their destruction caused Politian, and which drew from him the following epigram :—

Πολλάκι τοξευθεὶς φλεχθέις θ' ὑπὸ Πίκος ἐρώτων
  Οὐκ ἔτλη προτέρω, πάντα δ'ἀφείλεθ' ὅπλα,
Τόξα, βέλη, φαρέτρας, καὶ νήσας τά γε πάντα
  Ἦψεν ὁμοῦ σωρὸν λαμπάσι ληϊδίοις.
Σὺν δ'αὐτοὺς μάρψας ἀμεννὰ χερύδρια δῆσεν
  Ταῖς νευραῖς, μέσσῃ δ' ἔμβαλε πυρκαϊᾷ.
Καὶ πυρὶ φλέξε τὸ πῦρ· τί δ ὦ ἄφρονες αὐτὸν ἔρωτες
  Τὸν Πίκον μουσῶν εἰσεποτᾶσθε πρόμον ;

Ficino took a different view from Politian. " Somewhat of love," he wrote after Pico's death, " he had written in the heat of his youth, which in his riper judgment he condemned and determined altogether to destroy, nor could it have been published without damage to his reputation." This, however, probably refers not so much to the literary merit of the poems as to their moral tone. His nephew, Giovanni Francesco Pico distinctly states that they were destroyed "religionis causa." It is evident also from the way in which Politian refers to them that they were such as a less severe moralist than Ficino might have censured. "I hear," he wrote, "that you have burned the little love poems which you made in the past, fearing perhaps lest they should injure your fair fame or the morals of others. For I cannot think that you have destroyed them, as Plato is said to have destroyed his, because they were not worthy of publication. For as far as I remember nothing could be more terse, more sweet or more polished." Pico was wont to solace himself with Propertius, and had wantoned with other ladies than the Muses, so that in all likelihood his love poetry was decidedly more ardent than chaste. More (p. 13 *infra*) is inaccurate in stating that the " five books " thus destroyed were in the vulgar tongue. They were written, as we learn from Giovanni Francesco Pico "elegiaco carmine," *i.e.* in Latin elegies, probably modelled on Propertius. The Italian poems, however, were destroyed at the same time. Of Pico's Latin elegiacs two specimens survive : (1) a hymn to God written probably after his conversion ; (2) an encomiastic poem on his friend Girolamo Benivieni. For the first no high merit can be claimed. The attempt to give poetical expression to the mysteries of Christian theology is nearly always unsuccessful, and Pico's " Deprecatoria " forms no exception to the rule. The most that can be said for it is that it is tolerable Latin. Such as it is, however, it is here printed for comparison with More's translation, which will be found at page 74 *infra*.

JOANNIS PICI MIRANDULÆ DEPRECATORIA AD DEUM.

Alme Deus ! summa qui majestate verendus,
    Vere unum in triplici numine numen habes :
Cui super excelsi flammantia mœnia mundi
    Angelici servit turba beata chori :
Cujus et immensum hoc oculis spectabile nostris
    Omnipotens quondam dextra creavit opus :
Æthera qui torques, qui nutu dirigis orbem,
    Cujus ab imperio fulmina missa cadunt :
Parce, precor, miseris, nostras, precor, ablue sordes,
    Ne nos justa tui pœna furoris agat.
Quod si nostra pari pensentur debita lance
    Et sit judicii norma severa tui,
Quis queat horrendum viventis ferre flagellum
    Vindicis, et plagas sustinuisse graves ?
Non ipsa iratæ restabit Machina dextræ,
    Machina supremo non peritura die.
Quæ mens non primæ damnata ab origine culpæ,
    Aut quæ non proprio crimine facta nocens ?
Ast certe ille ipse es proprium cui parcere semper,
    Justitiamque pari qui pietate tenes :
Præmia qui ut meritis longe maiora rependis,
    Supplicia admissis sic leviora malis.
Namque tua est nostris major clementia culpis,
    Et dare non dignis res mage digna Deo est.
Quamquam sat digni, si quos dignatur amare
    Qui quos non dignos invenit ipse facit.
Ergo tuos placido miserans, precor, aspice vultu,
    Seu servos mavis, seu magis esse reos :
Nempe reos, nostræ si spectes crimina vitæ,
    Ingratæ nimium crimina mentis opus :
At tua si potius in nobis munera cernas,
    Munera præcipuis nobilitata bonis,
Nos sumus ipsa olim tibi quos natura ministros
    Mox fecit natos gratia sancta tuos.

Sed premit heu ! miseros tantæ indulgentia sortis,
　　Quos fecit natos gratia, culpa reos.
Culpa reos fecit, sed vincat gratia culpam,
　　Ut tuus in nostro crimine crescat honor.
Nam tua sive aliter sapientia, sive potestas,
　　Nota suas mundo prodere possit opes,
Major in erratis bonitatis gloria nostris,
　　Illeque præ cunctis fulget amandus amor,
Qui potuit cœlo Dominum deducere ab alto,
　　Inque crucem summi tollere membra Dei :
Ut male contractas patrio de semine sordes
　　Ablueret lateris sanguis et unda tui :
Sic amor et pietas tua, Rex mitissime, tantis
　　Dat mala materiem suppeditare bonis.
O amor ! O pietas nostris bene provida rebus !
　　O bonitas servi facta ministra tui !
O amor ! O pietas nostris male cognita sæclis !
　　O bonitas nostris nunc prope victa malis !
Da, precor, huic tanto qui semper fervet amori
　　Ardorem in nostris cordibus esse parem :
Da Sathanæ imperium, cui tot servisse per annos
　　Pœnitet excusso deposuisse jùgo :
Da, precor, extingui vesanæ incendia mentis,
　　Et tuus in nostro pectore vivat amor :
Ut cum mortalis perfunctus munere vitæ
　　Ductus erit Dominum spiritus ante suum,
Promissi regni felici sorte potitus
　　Non Dominum sed Te sentiat esse Patrem.

The poem on Benivieni is in a happier vein :—

Lætor, io, Tyrrhena, tibi, Florentia, lætor !
　　Clamet, io Pæan, quisquis amicus adest !
Quale decus, quæ fama, tibi, quæ gloria surgit !
　　Tolle caput, Libycas tolle superba jubas !
Ille tuos agros intra et tua mœnia natus,
　　Atque Arni liquidas inter adultus aquas,
Cui cum divinum sit sacro in pectore numen
　　Quam bene de sacro nomine nomen habet !
Ille, inquam, plausu jam cœpit ubique frequenti,
　　Jam cœpit multo non sine honore legi.
Sicelis Ausonias illius Musa per urbes
　　Fert celebrem magna candida laude pedem.

Auctorem patriæ quisquis legit invidet illi,
  Atque optat patriæ nomina tanta suæ.
Gaude, gaude iterum tanto insignita decore,
  Et vati adplaudas terra beata tuo.
Cinge coronatos vernanti flore capillos,
  Conveniunt titulo Florida serta tuo.
Undique Achæmenio spargantur compita costo,
  Et per odoratas lilia multa vias.
En ! stirps in nostras Benivenia protulit auras
  Etruscum docto qui gerat ore senem !
Ponite Avernales jam gens Etrusca cupressus,
  Quas rapta immiti funere Laura dedit.
Pellantur queruli fletus ; en ! Laura revixit ;
  Spirat ; et argutum novit, ut ante, loqui.
Quin solito nitet illa magis, majorque priore
  Nescio quæ cultu gratia ab ore venit.
Reddidit hanc nobis laus nostræ Hieronimus urbis,
  Et dedit infernos posse iterare lacus :
At certe (procul hinc O Livor inique facessas)
  Nunc graviore sonat grandius illa chely.
Di Superi ! sublime ales modulatur, ut æqua
  Sit jam Romano Tusca loquela sono.
Nec tamen ille Euros frondosus jactat inanes :
  Plus quam promittit fronte recessus habet.
Quid referam, quam lenis erat ? quam carmina plano
  In numeros currunt ordine juncta suos :
Sic memini me sæpe sacros vidisse liquores
  Profluere, imbriferi vis ubi nulla Noti.
Sed quis miretur meditato in carmine tantum
  Cultus, cum pariter non meditata canat ?
Quis non hunc juret Phœbum, modo pendeat arcus ?
  Cornua sint, Bromium quis neget esse Deum ?
Audivi hunc quoties cithara cantare recurva,
  Abduxit sensus protinus ille meos.
Et quid non possent digiti mulcere loquentis ?
  Sisteret his rapidi flumina magna Padi :
Phœbeos medio firmaret in æthere currus :
  Lunares pictos sisteret axe boves.
Terribilem sævis Martem revocaret ab armis :
  Leniret Ditem, falciferumque senem :
Et quas non potuit quondam Rhodopeius Orpheus
  Flectere Strymonias flecteret ille nurus.

The poem was apparently written after the death of Lorenzo, whose successor Pico hails in Benivieni. The epithet "Sicelis," applied to Benivieni's muse, refers to his bucolics; one of which (in praise of poetry) is entitled "Lauro," after Lorenzo; in another, which bears the name of "Pico," Lorenzo and Pico converse in amœbean strains. "Laura" stands apparently for Lorenzo's muse. "Etruscum qui gerat ore senem," is an uncouth and somewhat obscure phrase. "Nec tamen ille Euros frondosus jactat inanes" is plainly corrupt, but it is not easy to suggest a satisfactory emendation. "Quid referam, quam lenis *erat ?*" is too bad Latin to have been written by Pico. Perhaps the true reading is "quam lene sonet." The verses are undeniably spirited, though somewhat too rhetorical for true poetry.

It is, indeed, only as a rhetorician that Pico can claim to have succeeded. The letter to Ermolao Barbaro in defence of the schoolmen, and that to Lorenzo in praise of his verses are admirable examples of the rhetorical exercise pure and simple — for as such they must primarily be regarded—a little too elaborate, perhaps, too artificial, too declamatory, but still decidedly meritorious in their kind. The air of sincerity they certainly have not—indeed the scholastics of Padua were so far from taking Pico's eloquent panegyric of their predecessors seriously that they were inclined to suspect him of laughing at them in his sleeve. Nor is it easy to believe that Pico was really sincere in the exaggerated encomium which he passed on the verses of Lorenzo, one of the most insipid writers which even that age of learned insipidity produced. The real man, however, undoubtedly speaks in the letters on the philosophic and Christian life, the latter written, it must be remembered, when Pico was solemnized by the recent death of Lorenzo. The minor letters exhibit Pico in the pleasant light of the scholar writing to his friends to give or solicit information on various literary questions. One closes them, however, with a sigh of regret that the scholar should predominate so much over the man.

How thankful we should have been for a few easy gossiping letters in the vulgar tongue revealing Pico to us as he was in his moments of complete *abandon*. Perhaps, however, he knew none such, and there was nothing to reveal that he has not revealed. Sense of humour he seems certainly to have lacked; I have not found in him the least suggestion that he had any faculty of hearty laughing in him at all. If he ever had it, severe study must have crushed it out of him. Probably the basis of his nature was a deep religious melancholy, not at all lightened by the fact that learning had impaired his hold on the faith.

As his short life drew towards its close Pico's preoccupation with religion became more intense and exclusive. Besides the " Rules " of a Christian Life, and the " Interpretation " of Psalm XVI., translated by More, he wrote an Exposition of the Lord's Prayer, and projected, but did not live to execute a Commentary on the New Testament, for which he prepared himself by diligent collation of such MSS. as he could come by ; also a defence of the Vulgate and of the Septuagint version of the Psalms against the criticisms of the Jewish scholars, and an elaborate apology for Christianity against seven classes of opponents ; to wit (1) atheists, (2) idolators, (3) Jews, (4) Mahometans, (5) Christians who reject a portion of the faith, (6) Christians who adulterate the faith with profane superstitions, (7) orthodox Chris-

tians who live unholy lives.   Some idea of the scale of
this vast undertaking may be gathered from the fact that
the treatise "Adversus Astrologos," which occupies 240
closely printed folio pages formed only a small fragment
of it.

But while thus zealous for the defence of the faith,
Pico seems never to have seriously contemplated entering
the Church, though often urged to do so not only by
Savonarola but by other of his friends, who thought
he might reasonably aspire to the dignity of cardinal.
Their solicitude for his advancement he rebuked with
a haughty "Non sunt cogitationes meæ cogitationes
vestræ."   Probably he considered that he could render
religion truer service in the character of lay advocate
than if he were trammelled by clerical offices.

Short as his life was, he survived his three most inti-
mate friends, Lorenzo de' Medici, Ermolao Barbaro, and
Politian, all of whom died within the two years 1492-4.
Probably the grief caused by this succession of mis-
fortunes had much to do with inducing or aggravating
the fever of which he died hardly two months after
Politian, on 17th Nov. 1494.   The corpse, invested
by Savonarola's own hands with the habit of the order of
the Frati Predicanti, in which he had ardently desired to
enrol Pico during his life, was buried in the church of S.
Marco.   The tomb was inscribed with the epitaph :

"Joannes jacet hic Mirandula : cætera norunt
Et Tagus, et Ganges, forsan et Antipodes."

Ficino, who had been to him "in years as a father, in
intimacy as a brother, in affection as a second self," wrote
another epitaph, which was not, however, placed upon
the tomb : "Antistites secretiora mysteria raro admodum

concedunt oculis, statimque recondunt. Ita Deus mortalibus divinum philosophum Joannem Picum Mirandulam trigesimo (*sic*) anno maturum."

The generous enthusiasm which prompted Politian to confer upon his friend the high-sounding title of "Phœnix of the wits" (Fenice degli ingegni) has not been justified by events. Once sunk in his ashes the Phœnix never rose again.

The pious care of Giovanni Francesco Pico, who published his uncle's life and works at Venice in 1498, did much, indeed, to avert the oblivion which ultimately fell upon him. This edition, however, was imperfect, the Theses and the Commentary on Benivieni's poem, with some minor matters being omitted. These were added in the Basel edition of 1601. The "Golden Letters" have passed through many editions, the last that of Cellario in 1682. The Commentary on Celestial and Divine Love was reprinted as late as 1731.

Pico figures in a dim and ever dimmer way in the older histories of philosophy from Stanley, who gives a rude and imperfect translation of the "Commentary" to Hegel, who dismisses him and his works in a few lines. More recently, however, one of Hegel's laborious fellow-countrymen, Georg Dreydorff, discovered a system in Pico and expounded it.[1]

But most Englishmen probably owe such interest as he excites in them to Mr. Pater's charming sketch in his dainty volume of studies entitled "The Renaissance," or the slighter notices in Mr. J. A. Symonds' "Renaissance in Italy," or Mr. Seebohm's "Oxford Reformers."

The Life by Sir Thomas More now reprinted is a

[1] "Das System des Johann Pico Grafen von Mirandula und Concordia," *Marburg*, 1858.

somewhat reduced and inaccurate version of Giovanni Francesco Pico's work. The reprint is executed from a small black-letter quarto in the British Museum, printed by Wynkyn de Worde about 1510. The old spelling and, as far as possible, the old punctuation has been retained, though in many places it has been necessary to alter the latter in order to avoid intolerable harshness or obscurity.

The chronicles of Mirandola, edited for the municipality in 1872, under the title " Memorie Storiche della Città e dell' Antico Ducato della Mirandola," are an authority of capital importance for the history of the Pico family and its connexions. The notes to Riccardo Bartoli's " Elogio al Principe Pico" (1791) also contain some valuable original matter. The critical judgment of the last century on Pico's services to the cause of the revival of learning is given by Christoph Meiners in " Lebensbeschreibungen berühmter Männer der Wiederherstellung der Wissenschaften." Some of Pico's letters translated, into the ponderous English of the period, connected by a thread of biography, and illustrated by erudite notes, will be found in W. Parr Greswell's " Memoirs of Angelus Politianus," etc. 1805. The best modern Italian biography is that by F. Calori Cesis, entitled " Giovanni Pico della Mirandola detto La Fenice degli Ingegni" (2nd edn. 1872).

HERE IS CONTEYNED THE LYFE OF JOHAN PICUS
ERLE OF MYRANDULA A GRETE LORDE OF
ITALY AN EXCELLENT CONNYNGE MAN IN ALL
SCIENCES & VERTEOUS OF LYVYNGE. WITH
DYVERS EPYSTLES & OTHER WERKES OF Y^E
SAYD JOHAN PICUS FULL OF GRETE SCIENCE
VERTUE & WYSEDOME WHOSE LIFE &
WERKES BENE WORTHY & DYGNE
TO BE REDDE AND OFTEN
TO BE HAD IN
MEMORYE.

B

UNTO HIS RYGHT ENTYERLY BELOVED SYSTER IN CHRYST JOYEUCE LEYGH[1] THOMAS MORE GRETYNG IN OUR LORDE.

IT is and of longe tyme hath bene my well beloved fyster a cuftome in the begynnynge of y^e newe yere frendes to fende betwene prefentes or gyftes, as the wytneffes of theyr love and frende fhyp & alfo fygnyfyenge that they defyre eche to other that yere a good contynuance and profperous ende of that lucky bygynnynge. But communely all thofe prefentes that are ufed cuftomably all in this maner betwene frendes to be fente be fuche thynges as pertayne onely unto the body eyther to be fed or to be cledde or fome otherwyfe delyted : by whiche hit femeth that theyr frendfhyp is but flefshely & ftretcheth in maner to the body onely. But for afmoche as the love & amyte of chryften folke fholde be rather goofty frendfhyp then bodely : fyth y^t all faythfull people are rather fpyrituall then carnall : for as th'apoftle feyth we be not now in flefshe but in fpyryte yf Chryfte abyde in us : I therfore myne hertly beloved fyfter in good lucke of this newe yere have fent you fuche a prefent as maye bere wytnes of my tendre love & zele to the happy contynuaunce and gracyoufe encreace of vertue in your foule : and where as

3

the giftes of other folke declare y‘ they wyfsheth theyr frendes to be worldly fortunate, myne teſtyfyeth y‘ I de-fyre to have you godly profperous.   Thefe werkes more profitable then large were made in laten by one Johan Picus Erle of Mirandula a lordſhyp in Italy, of whose connynge & vertue we nede here nothinge to fpeke, for afmoche as here after we perufe the courfe of his hole lyfe rather after our lytel power flenderly then after his merites fuffyciently. The werkes are fuche that truely good fyſter I fuppofe of the quantyte there cometh none in your hand more pro-fitable : neyther to th'achyvynge of temperaunce in pro-fperite, nor to y° purchafynge of pacience in adverſite, nor to the dyfpyfynge of worldly vanyte, nor to the de-fyrynge of hevenly felycyte: whiche werkes I wolde requyre you gladly to receyve : ne were hit y‘ they be fuche that for the goodly mater (how fo ever they be tranflated) may delyte & pleafe ony perfone that hath ony meane defyre and love to God: and that your felfe is fuche one as for your vertue and fervent zele to God can not but joyoufly receyve ony thynge that meanely fowneth eyther to the reproche of vyce, commendacyon of vertue, or honoure and laude of God, who preferve you.

THE LYFE OF JOHAN PICUS, ERLE OF MIRANDULA.

OHAN PICUS OF THE faders[2] fyde defcended of the worthy lynage of th'emperoure Conftantyne by a nevew of the fayd Emperour called Picus, by whom all the Aunceftres of this Johan Picus undoubtedly bere that name. But we fhal let his aunceftres paffe, to whome (though they were ryght excellent) he gave agayne as moche honour as he receyved. And we fhal fpeke of hym felfe reherfynge in parte his lernynge and his vertue. For thefe be the thynges whiche maye accompte for our owne, of whiche every man is more proprely to be commended then of y[e] noblenes of his aunceftres : whofe honoure maketh us not honorable. For eyther they were them felfe vertuoufe or not : yf not, then had they none honour them felfe had they never fo grete poffeffyons : for honoure is the rewarde of vertue. And how may they clayme the rewarde y[t] proprely longeth to vertue : yf they lak the vertue that y[e] rewarde longeth to. Then yf them felfe had none honour : how myght they leve to theyr heyres y[t] thynge whiche they had not them felfe. On y[e] other fyde yf they be vertuous and fo confequently

5

honorable, yet maye they not leve theyr honoure to us as enheretaunce : no more then the vertue that them felfe were honourable for. For never the more noble be we for theyr noblenes : yf our felfe lak thofe thynges for which they were noble. But rather the more worfhipful that our aunceftres were, the more vile and fhamfull be we : yf we declyne from y⁰ fteppes of theyr worfhypfull lyvynge : y⁰ clere beauty of whofe vertue makith the darke fpotte of our vyce the more evydently to appere and to be y⁰ more marked. But Picus of whom we fpeke was him felfe fo honorable, for y⁰ grete plentuoufe habundaunce of all fuche vertues, y⁰ poffeffyon wherof very honoure foloweth (as a fhadowe folowith a body) yᵗ he was to all them yᵗ afpyre to honour a very fpeˊtacle, in whofe condycyons as in a clere pullifhed myrrour they myght beholde in what poyntes very honour ftondeth : whofe merveylous connynge & excellent vertue though my rude lernynge be ferre unable fuffyciently to ex-preffe : yet for as moche as yf no man fholde do hit but he yᵗ might fufficiently do hit, no man fholde do hit : & better it were to be unfufficiently done then utterly un-done : I fhal therfore as I can brefely reherfe you his hole lyfe : at the leeft wyfe to gyve fome other man here after (yᵗ can do hit better) occafyon to take hit in hande when hit fhall happely greve hym to fe the lyfe of fuche an excellent connyng man fo ferre unkonnyngly wryten.

OF HIS PARENTES AND
TYME OF HIS BYRTH.

In y⁰ yere of our Lorde God . M . CCCC . lxiii . Pius the feconde beynge than the generall vycare of Chryfte in his chyrche : and Frederyk the thyrde of yᵗ name rulynge the empyre : this noble man was borne the laft chylde of

6

his mother ·Julya, a woman comen of a noble ftok,[3] his father hyght Johan Fauncife, a lorde of grete honoure and auctorite.

OF THE WONDRE THAT APPERED
BEFORE HIS BYRTH.

A merveyloufe fyght was there fcene before his byrthe : there appered a fyery garlande ftandynge over y[e] chaumbre of his mother whyle fhe travelled & fodenly vanyfshed away : which apparence was peradventure a token that he whiche fholde y[t] houre in the companye of mortall men be borne in the perfeccion of underftandynge fholde be lyke y[e] perfyte fygure of that rounde cyrcle or garlande: and that his excellent name fholde rounde aboute the cyrcle of this hole world be magnyfyed, whofe mynde fholde alway as the fyre afpyre upwarde to hevenly thynge, and whofe fyry eloquence fholde with an ardent hert in tyme to come whorfhip and prayfe almighty God with all his ftrength : and as that flame fodenly vanifshyd fo fholde this fyre fone frome y[e] eyen of mortal people be hydde. We have oftyntymes red that fuche unknowen and ftraunge tokens hathe gone before or foloweth the na-tyvytefe of excellente wyfe and vertuoufe men, departynge (as hit were) and by Goddes commaundement feverynge the cradyls of fuche fpecyall chyldren fro y[e] company of other of the comune forte : and fhewynge y[t] they be borne to the acchevynge of fome grete thyng. But to paffe over other. The grete Saynt Ambrofe : a fwarme of bees flewe aboute his mouth in his cradle, & fome entred in to his mouthe, and after y[t] yffuynge out agayne and fleynge up on hyghe, hydynge them felfe amonge the cloudes, efcaped bothe y[e] fyght of his father and of all them that were prefent: whiche pronoftycacyon one

7

Paulinus [4] makynge moche of, expowned it to fignyfye to us the fwete hony combes of his plefaunt wrytynge: whiche fholde fhewe out the celeftiall gyftes of God & fholde lyfte up the mynde of men from erthe in to heven.

OF HIS PERSONE.

He was of feture and fhappe femely and beauteous, of ftature goodly and hyghe, of flefshe tendre and fofte: his vyfage lovely and fayre, his coloure white entermengled with comely ruddes, his eyen gray and quicke of loke, his teth white and even, his heere yelowe and not to piked.[5]

OF HIS SETTYNGE FORTHE TO SCOLE AND STUDY IN HUMANTYE.

Under y[e] rule and governaunce of his mother he was fet to mayfters & to lernynge: where with fo ardent mynde. he labored the ftudyes of humanite: y[t] within fhorte whyle he was (and not without a caufe) accompted amonge the chyef Oratours and Poetes of that tyme: in lernynge mervayloufly fwyfte and of fo redy a wyt, that y[e] verfis whiche he herde ones red he wolde agayne bothe forwarde and bakwarde to the grete wonder of the herers reherfe, and over that wolde holde hit in fure remembraunce: whiche in other folkes wonte comenly to happen contrary. For they y[t] are fwyfte in takyng be oftentymes flowe in remembrynge, and they y[t] with more labour & dyffyculte receyve hit more faft & fuerely holde hit.

OF HIS STUDY IN CANONE.

In the fouretene yere of his age by the commaundement of his mother (whiche longed vere fore to have hym preeft) he departed to Bononye to ftudy in y[e] lawes of the chyrche, whiche whan he had two yere tafted, per-

8

ceyvynge that the faculte leyned to nothinge but onely mery tradicions and ordinaunces, his mynde fyll frome hit : yet loft he not his tyme therin, for in that two yere yet beynge a chylde he compyled a brevyary or a fumme upon all the decretalles, in whiche as brefly as poffyble was he compryfed th' effecte of all y^t hole grete volume, and made a boke no fclender thyng to ryght connyng & perfyte doctours.

OF HIS STUDY IN PHYLOSOPHYE & DEVYNYTE.

After this as a defyrous enferchour of the fecretes of nature he lefte thefe commyn troden pathes and gave hym felfe hole to fpeculation & philofophy as well humane as devyne. For the purchafynge wherof (afte the maner of Plato and Appollonius) [6] he fcrupuloufly fought out all the famous doctours of his tyme, vifytynge ftudeoufly all the unyverfytes and fcoles not onely through Italy but alfo through Fraunce. And fo infatigable laboure gave he to thofe ftudies : that yet a chylde and berdles he was bothe reputed and was in dede bothe a perfyte philofophre and a perfyte devyne.

OF HIS MYNDE AND VAYNGLORYOUSE DISPICIONS OF ROME.

Now had he ben. vii. yere converfaunt in thefe ftudies whan full of pryde & defyrous of glory and mannes prayfe (for yet was he not kendled in ye love of God) he went to Rome, and there (covetynge to make a shew of his connynge : & lytel confideringe how grete envye he fholde reyfe agaynft hym felfe) ix. C. queftions he purpofed, of dyverfe & fondry maters : as well in logike and philofophye as dyvynyte with grete ftudy piked and fought

out as well of the laten auctours as the Grekes : and partly
fet oute of the fecrete mifteryes of the Hebrewes, Caldeyes,
& Arabies : and many thynges drawen out of y⁰ olde obfcure philofophye of Pythagoras, Trimegiftus, and Orpheus,⁷
& many other thynges ftraunge : and to all folke (except
ryght fewe fpecyall excellente men) before that daye : not
unknowen onely: but alfo unherde of. All whiche queftions
in open places (y' they myght be to all people y⁰ better
knowen) he faftened and fet up, offeryng alfo hym felfe
to bere the coftes of all fuche as wolde come hyther out
of ferre countrees to dyfpute, but thorughe y⁰ envye of
his malicyous enemyes (which envye lyke y⁰ fyre ever
draweth to y⁰ hygheft) he coude never brynge a boute to
have a day to his dyfpicions appoynted. For this caufe
he taryed at Rome an hole yere, in all which tyme his
envyours never durfte openly with open difpicyons at-
empt hym, but rather with crafte and fleyght and as it
were with pryvey trenches enforced to under myne hym,
for none other caufe but for malice and for they were (as
many men thought) corrupte with a peftylent envye.

This envye as men demed was fpecyaly rayfed agaynft
hym for this caufe that where there were many whiche had
many yeres: fome for glory : fome for couetyfe : gyven
them felfe to lernynge : they thought that hit fholde
happely deface theyr fame & minyfshe th'opynyon of
theyr connynge yf fo yonge a man plenteoufe of fubftaunce & greate doctryne durfte in the chyefe cyte of
the worlde make a profe of his wyt and his lernyng : as
well in thinges naturall as in divinite & in many fuche
thynges as men many yeres never attayned to. Nowe
when they perceyved that they coude not agaynft his
connynge ony thynge openly preuayle, they brought
forth the ferpentynes of falfe crime, and cryed out that

there wer. xiij. of his. ix. C. queſtyons ſuſpecte of heryſye. Then joyned they to them ſome good ſymple folke that ſholde of zele to yᵉ fayth and pretence of relygion impugne thoſe queſtions as newe thynges & with whiche theyr eres had not be in ure. In whiche impugnacyon though ſome of theym happely lacked not good mynde : yet lacked they erudycyon and lernynge : whiche queſtyons notwitſtondynge before that not a fewe famous doctours of divynyte had approved as good and clene, and ſubſcribed theyr names undre them. But he not berynge the loſſe of his fame made a defence for. thoſe xiij. queſtyons : a werke of greate erudicyon and elegant and ſtuffed with the cognytyon of many thynges worthy to be lerned. Whiche werke he compyled in xx nyghtes. In whiche hit evedently appereth : not onely that thoſe concluſyons were good and ſtondyng with the fayth : but alſo yᵗ they whiche had barked at theym were of foly and rudeneſſe to be reproved : whiche defence and all other thynges that he ſholde wryte he commytted lyke a good chryſten man to yᵉ moſt holy judgement of our mother holy chyrche : whiche defence receyved : & yᵉ xiij. queſtions duly by delyberacyon examyned : our holy father yᵉ pope approved Picus and tenderly favoured hym, as by a bull of our holy father pope Alexandre the vj, hit playnly appereth : but the boke in whiche the hole. ix. C. queſtions with theyr concluſions were conteyned (for as moche as there were in them many thynges ſtraunge and not fully declared, and were more mete for ſecrete communycacyon of lerned men then for open herynge of commune people, whiche for lacke of connynge myght take hurte therby) Picus deſyred hym ſelfe yᵗ hit ſholde not be redde. And ſoo was the redynge therof forboden. Lo this ende had Picus of his hye mynde and proud purpofe, that where he thought to have goten perpetual prayfe there had he moche werke to kepe hymfelfe upryght : that he ranne not in perpetual infamye and fclaundre.

OF THE CHAUNGE OF HIS LYFE.

But as hym felfe tolde his nevewe he judged y' this came thus to paffe : by the efpeciall provifion and fynguler goodnes of almyghty God, that by this fals cryme untruely put upon hym by his evyll wyllers he sholde correcte his very errours, and that this fholde be to hym (wanderynge in derkenes) as a fhynynge lyght : in whiche he myght beholde & confydre : how ferre he had gone out of ye waye of trouth. For before this he had bene bothe defyrous of glory and kyndled in vayne love and holden in volupteoufe ufe of women. The comelynes of his body with the lovely favoure of his vyfage, and therwith all his merveyloufe fame, his excellent lernynge, grete rycheffe and noble kyndred, fet many women a fyre on hym, frome ye defyre of whome he not abhorrynge (ye waye of lyfe fet a fyde) was fom what fallen in to wantonneffe. But after that he was ones with this variaunce wakened he drewe backe his mynde flowynge in riot & turned hit to Chryft, womens blandimentes he chaunged into ye defyre of hevenly joyes, & difpifynge the blafte of vaynglorye which he before defyred, now with all his mynde he began to feke the glory and profytè of Chryftes chyrche, and fo began he to ordre his condycions y^t from thens forth he myght have ben approved & thoughe his enemye were his judge.

OF THE FAME OF HIS VERTUE AND THE RESORTE UNTO HYM THERFORE.

Here upon fhortly the fame of his noble connynge and

excellent vertue bothe ferre & nygh began gloryoufly to
fprynge for which many worthy philofophres (& that
were taken in nombre of the mooft connynge) reforted
bifely unto hym as to a market of good doctryne, fome
for to move queftions and dyfpute, fome (that were of
more godly mynde) to here and to take the holefome
leffons and inftruccyon of good lyvynge : whiche leffons
were fo moche y⁰ more fet by : in how moche they came
from a more noble man and a more wyfe man and hym
alfo whiche had hym felfe fome tyme folowed y⁰ croked
hilles of delycyoufe pleafure. To the faftenynge of good
dyfcyplyne in the myndes of y⁰ herers those thynges feme
to be of grete effecte : whiche be bothe of theyr owne
nature good & alfo be fpoken of fuche a mafter as is
converted to the way of juftyce from the croked & ragged
path of voluptuoufe lyvynge.

THE BURNYNG OF WANTON BOKES.

Fyve bokes that in his youthe of wanton verfis of love
with other lyke fantafies he had made in his vulgar
tongue : all togyther (in deteftacyon of his vyce paffed)
and left thefe tryfles myght be fome evyll occafyon afterwarde, he burned them.

OF HIS STUDY AND DILYGENCE
IN HOLY SCRYPTURE.

From thensforth he gave him felfe day & nyght mooft
fervently to the ftudyes of fcrypture, in whiche he wrote
many noble bokes : whiche well teftyfye bothe his angylyke
wyt, his ardent laboure, and his profounde erudicyon, of
whiche bokes some we have & fome as an ineftimable
treafure we have lofte. Grete lybraries hit is incredible
to confydre with how merveloufe celeryte he red them

over, and wrote out what hym liked : of yᵉ olde fathers of yᵉ chyrch, fo gret knowlege he had as hit were harde for hym to have yᵗ hath lyved longe & all his lyfe hath done nothyng els but red them. Of thefe newer dyvynes fo good jugement he had yᵗ it myght appere there were nothynge in ony of them yᵗ were unknowen to him, but all thynge as rype as though he had all theyr werkes ever before his eyen, but of all thefe new doctours he fpecyally commendeth Saynt Thomas[8] as hym yᵗ enforfeth hym felfe in a fure piller of truth. He was very quick, wife, & fubtyl in difpicions & had grete felicite therin while he had yᵗ hye ftomak. But now a grete while he had bode fuche conflictes farewell : and every daye more & more hated them, and fo gretely abhored them that when Hercules Eftenfis Duke of Ferrare[9] : fyrft by meffengers and after by hym felfe : defyred hym to difpute at Ferrare : bycaufe the generall chapytre of freres prechours was holden there : longe hit was or he coude be brought therto : but at the inftant requeft of the Duke whiche very fyngulerly loved him he came thyder, where he fo behaved hym felfe yᵗ was wondre to beholde how all yᵉ audyence rejoyced to here hym, for hit were not poffyble for a man to utter neyther more connynge nor more connyngely. But hit was a commune fayenge with hym yᵗ fuche altercacyons were for a logition and not metely for a phylofophre, he fayd also that suche difputacyons gretely profited as were exercifed with a peafyble mynde to th'enferchynge of the treuth in fecrete company without grete audyence : but he fayd that thofe difpicions dyd grete hurte yᵗ were holden openly to th'oftentacion of lernynge & to wynne the favoure of the commune people & the commendacyon of fooles. He thought that utterly hit coulde unneth be but that with the defyre of worfhyp (whiche thefe gafynge

dyſputers gape after) there is with an inſeparable bonde
annexed the appetite of his confuſyon & rebuke whome
they argue with, whiche appetyte is a dedly wounde to yᵉ
ſoule, & a mortall poyſon to charite.   There was nothing
paſſed hym of thoſe capicions ſoteltes & cavilacions of
ſophyſtrye, nor agayn there was nothyng yᵗ he more
hated & abhored, conſyderyng that they ſerved of nought
but to yᵉ ſhamyng of ſuche other folke as were in very
ſcyence moche better lerned and in thoſe trifles ignoraunt :
and yᵗ unto th'enſercherchynge of yᵉ treuth (to which he
gave contynuall laboure) they profyted lytell or nought.

OF HIS LERNYNGE UNYVERSALLY.

But bycauſe we wyll holde the reder no longer in hande :
we wyll ſpeke of his lernynge but a worde or twayne
generally. Some man hathe ſhyned in eloquence, but ignorance of naturall thynges hathe diſhoneſted hym.   Some
man hath floured in the knowledge of dyvers ſtraunge
languages, but he hath wanted all the cognicion of philo-
ſophye. Some man hath redde the invencyons of the
olde philoſophres, but he hath not ben exerciſed in the
new ſcoles. Some man hath ſought connynge as well
philoſophie as dyvinite for prayſe and vayneglorye and
not for ony profyte or encreace of Chryſtes chyrche. But
Pycus all theſe thynges with equall ſtudy hath ſo receyved
yᵗ they myght ſeme by hepis as a plentyouſe ſtreme to
have flowen in to hym.   For he was not of yᵉ condycion
of ſome folke (which to be excellent in one thynge ſet al
other afyde) but he in all ſciences profyted ſo excellently :
that which of theym ſo ever he had conſydered, in him ye
wolde have thought yᵗ he had taken that one for his onely
ſtudye. And all theſe thynges were in hym ſo moche
the more merverlouſe in yᵗ he came therto by hym ſelfe

15

with y^e ſtrength of his owne wytte for the love of God and profyte his chyrche without mayſters, ſo that we may ſaye of hym that Epycure the philoſophre ſayd of hym that he was his owne mayſter.¹⁰

FYVE CAUSES Y^T IN SO SHORTE TYME BROUGHT HYM TO SE MERVELOUSE CONNYNGE.

To the bryngynge forth of ſo wondreful effectes in ſo ſmall tyme I confidre fyve cauſes to have come togyder: fyrſt an incredyble wyt, ſecondely a merveylouſe faſt memore, thyrdely grete ſubſtaunce by ye which to ye byenge of his bokes as wel laten as greke & other tonges he was eſpecyally holpen. vij.m. ducates he had layde out in the gaderynge to gyther of volumes of all maner of litterature. The fourth cauſe was his beſy and infatigable ſtudy. The fyſte was the contempt diſpyſynge of all erthly thynges.

OF HIS CONDYCYONS AND HIS VERTUE.

But now let us paſſe over thoſe powers of his ſoule which appertayne to underſtondynge & knowledge & let us ſpeke of them y^t belonge to ye achevynge of noble actes, let us as we can declare his excellent condicions y^t his mynde enflamed to Godwarde may appere, and his riches gyven out to poore folke may be underſtonde, th'entent y^t they whiche ſhall heere his vertue may have occaſyon therby to gyve eſpeciall laude & thanke to almyghty God, of whoſe infynyte goodneſſe all grace and vertue cometh.

OF THE SALE OF HIS LORDESHYPPES AND ALMYSSE.

Thre yere before his deth (to th'ende that all the charge

& befynes of rule or lordſhyp fet a fyde he myght lede his lyfe in reſt and peace, wele confyderynge to what ende this erthely honour & worldly dignite cometh) all his patrymonye and dominyons : y^t is to fay : the thyrde parte of th'erldome of Mirandula and of Concordia : unto Johan Francis his nevewe he folde, and that fo good chepe that hit femed rather a gyft then a fale." All that ever he receyved of this bargayne partly he gave out to poore folke, partely he beſtowed in ye byenge of a lytell londe, fyndynge of hym & his houſholde. And over y^t : moche fylver veſſell & plate with other precyoufe & coſtly uten-files of howſholde he devyded amonge poore people. He was content with meane fare at his table, how be hit fom-what yet reteynynge of ye olde plenty in deynty vyande & fylver veſſel. Every daye at certayne houres he gave hym felfe to prayer. To pore men alway yf ony came he plentiouſly gave out his money : & not content onely to gyve that he had hym felf redy : he wrote over y^t to one Hierom Benivenius [12] a florentin, a well letred man (whom for his grete love towarde hym & ye integrite of his con-dycions he fingulerly favored) y^t he ſholde with his owne money ever helpe poore folke : & gyve maydens money to theyre maryage : and alway fende him worde what he had layde out that he myght paye hit him ageyn. This offyce he commytted to hym that he might ye more eafely by hym as by a faythful meſſenger releve ye neceſſyte & miferi of poore nedy people fuche as hym felfe happely coude not come by ye knowlege of.

OF Y^E VOLUNTARY AFFLECCION & PAY-NING OF HIS OWN BODY.

Over all this : many times (whiche is not to be kepte fecrete) he gave almes of his owne body : we knowe many men which (as Saynt Hierom [13] fayth) put forth theyr hande to poore folke : but with the plefure of ye flesfhe they be overcomen : but he many days (and namely [14] thofe dayes whiche reprefent unto us ye paffyon & deth y^t Chryfte fuffred for our fake) bet and fcourged his owne flefhe in the remembraunce of that grete benefyte and for clenfynge of his olde offences.

OF HIS PLACABILITE OR BENYGNE NATURE.

He was of chere alwaye mery & of fo benygne nature y^t he was never troubled with angre & he fayd ones to his nevew that what fo ever fholde happen (fell ther never fo grete myfadventure) he coude never as hym thought be moved to wrath but yf his chyftes peryfshed in whiche his bokes laye y^t he had with grete trauayle & watche compiled : but for as moche as he confydered y^t he laboured onely for ye love of God & profyte of his chyrche : & y^t he had dedicate unto him all his werkes, his ftudyes & his doynges : & fith he fawe y^t fyth God is almyghty they coulde not mifcarye but yf it were eyther by his commaundement or by his fufferaunce : he veryly trufted : fyth God is all good : y^t he wolde not fuffre hym to have that occafion of hevynes. O very happy mynde which none adverfyte myght oppreffe, which no prof-peryte might enhaunce : not the connynge of all philo-fophie was able to make hym proude, not the know-ledge of the hebrewe, chaldey & arabie language befyde greke and laten coulde make hym vayngloryouse, not his grete fubftaunce, not his noble blode, coulde blowe up his herte, not ye beauty of his body, not ye grete occafyon of fynne were able to pull hym bak in to ye voluptuoufe brode way y^t ledeth to helle : what thynge was ther of fo mervayloufe ftrength y᷑ might overtorne y᷑ mynde of hym: which now (as Seneke fayth) was goten above fortune᷑ᶳ as he which as well her favoure as her malice hath fet at nought, y᷑ he myght be coupled with a fpiritull knot unto Chryfte and his hevenly cytezeynes.

HOW HE ESCHEWED DYGNITES.

Whan he fawe many men with grete labour & money defyre & byfely purchafe y᷑ offices & dygnites of y᷑ chirche (whiche are now a dayes alas y᷑ whyle communely bought & folde) him felfe refufed to recyve them whan two kynges offred them: whan an other man offred hym grete worldely promocyon yf he wolde go to y᷑ kynges courte: he gave hym fuche an anfwere, that he fholde well knowe that he neyther defyred worfhip ne worldly ryches but rather fet them at nought y᷑ he might y᷑ more quyetly gyve hym felfe to ftudy & y᷑ fervyce of God: this wyfe he perfuaded, y᷑ to a phylofophre and hym y᷑ feketh for wyfedome it was no prayfe to gather rycheffe but to refufe them.

OF THE DISPYSYNGE OF WORLDLY GLORYE.

All prayfe of people and all erthly glorye he reputed utterly for nothyng: but in y᷑ renayeng of this fhadowe of glory he laboured for very glorye which ever more foloweth vertue as an unfeparable fervaunt. He fayd that fame often tymes dyd hurte to men while they lyve, & never good whan they be deed. So moche onely fet he by his lernynge in how moche he knewe that hit was profytable to y᷑ chyrche & to y᷑ extermynation of errours. And over that: he was come to that prycke of perfyte humilite that he lytell forced wyther his workes went out under his owne name or not fo that they might as moche profite as yf they were gyven oute under his name. And nowe fet he lytel by ony other bokes fave onely ye bible, in y^c onely ftudi of which he had appoynted hym felfe to fpende the refedewe of his lyfe, favynge that ye commune profyte pricked him whan he confydered fo many & fo grete werkes as he had conceyved & longe travayled upon howe they were of every man by and by [16] defyred and loked after.

HOW MOCHE HE SET MORE BY DEVOCYON THAN CONNYNGE.

The lytell affeccyon of an olde man or an olde woman to Godwarde (were it never fo fmall) he fet more by : then by all his owne knowlege as well of naturall thynges as godly. And oftentymes in communicacyon he wolde admonyfshe his familyar frendes how gretly thefe mortall thynges bowe and drawe to an ende, howe flyper & how fallynge hit is y^t we lyve in now : how ferme how ftable it fhall be y^t we fhal here after lyve in, whether we be throwen downe in to hell or lyfte up in to heven. Wherfore he exhorted them to turne up theyr myndes to love God, which was a thynge farre excellynge all the connynge y^t is poffible for us in this lyfe to obtaine. The fame thynge alfo in his boke whiche he entytled De Ente et Uno lyghtfomely he treateth where he interupteth ye courfe of his difpicion and turnynge his wordes to Angelus Politianus (to whom he dedycateth that boke) he wryteth in this wyfe. But now beholde o my welbeloved Angell what madnes holdeth us. Love God (while we be in this body) we rather maye : than eyther knowe him or by fpeche utter hym. In lovyng him alfo we more profyte our felfe, we laboure leffe & ferve hym more, & yet had we lever alwaye by knowlege never fynde y^t thynge that

20

we feke : then by love to poffede y' thynge whiche alfo
without love were in vayne founde.[17]

OF HIS LIBERALITE & CONTEMPT OF RYCHESSE.

Liberalite onely in hym paffed meafure : for fo ferre was
he from y° begynnyng of ony diligence to erthely thynges
that he femed fom what befprent with the frekyll of
negligence. His frendes oftentymes admonyfhed hym that
he fholde not all utterly difpyce rycheffe, fhewynge hym
y' hit was his difhonefte and rebuke whan it was reported
(were it treue or falfe) that his negligence & fettyng
nought by money gave his fervauntes occafyon of difceyt
& robbry. Nevertheles that mynde of his (which evermore on hyghe cleved faft in contemplacion & in th'enferchynge of natures counfel) coulde never let downe hit
felfe to y° confideracion and overfeynge of thefe bafe
abjecte and vyle erthly tryfles. His hygh ftuarde came
on a tyme to hym & defyred hym to receyve his accomt
of fuche money as he had in many yeres receyved of
his : and brought forth his bokes of rekenynge. Picus
anfwered hym in this wyfe, my frende (fayth he) I knowe
well ye have mought oftentimes and yet may defceyve
me and ye lyft, wherfore the examinacyon of thefe ex-
penfes fhall not nede. There is no more to do, yf I be
ought in your det I fhall pay you by & by,[18] yf ye be in
myn pay me : eyther now yf ye have hit : or here after yf
ye be now not able.

OF HIS LOVYNGE MYNDE & VERTUOUSE BEHAVOUR TO HIS FRENDES.

His lovers and frendes with grete benygnite & curtefye
he entreted, whom he ufed in all fecrete comminge vertuoufly to exhorte to Godward, whofe goodely wordes fo

effectually wrought in ye herers y^t where a connynge
man (but not fo good as connynge) came to him on a
daye for ye grete fame of his lernyng to commune with
hym, as they fell in talkynge of vertue he was with the
wordes of Picus fo throughly perced that forth with all
he forfoke his accuftomed vyce and reformed his condicyons. The wordes y^t he fayd unto hym were thefe:
yf we hadde ever more before our eyen ye paynful deth
of Chryft which he fuffred for the love of us: and than
yf we wolde agayne thynke upon our deth: we fholde wele
beware of fynne. Merveyloufe benignyte & curtefy he
fhewed unto them: not whom ftrength of body or goodes
of fortune magnified but to them whom lernynge & condicions bounde hym to favoure: for fimylytude of maners
is a caufe of love & frendefhyp. A likenes of condicions
is (as Appollonius fayth) an affinyte.[19]

WHAT HE HATED AND WHAT HE LOVED.

There was nothyng more odioufe nor more intolirable to
hym than as (Horace [20] fayth) ye proud palaces of ftately
lordes: weddynge and worldly befynes he fled almooft a
lyke: notwithftondynge whan he was axed ones in fporte
whyther of thofe two burdeynes femed lyghter & whiche
he wolde chefe yf he fholde of neceffite be dryven to that
one and at his eleccyon: whiche he ftiked thereat a wyle
but at ye laft he fhoke his heed and a lytell fmylyng he
anfwered y^t he had lever take hym to maryage, as y^t
thynge in whiche was leffe fervytude & not fo moche
jeoperdy. Lyberte above all thynge he loved, to which
both his owne natural affeccon & ye ftudy of phylofophy
enclyned hym: & for y^t was he alwaye wanderyng &
flytynge & wolde never take hym felfe to ony certayne
dwellynge.[21]

Of outward obfervaunces he gave no very grete force : we fpeke not of thofe obfervaunces which the chyrche commaundeth to be obferved, for in thofe he was dilygent : but we fpeke of thofe cerymonyes which folke brynge up fettynge y⁰ very fervyce of God a fyde, which is (as Chryft fayth) to be worfhipped in fpirite & in treuth. But in the inwarde affectes of the mynde he cleved to God with very fervent love and devocyon : fome tyme that merveloufe alacrite langwyfshed and almooft fell, and efte agayne with grete ftrength rofe up in to God. In the love of whome he fo fervently burned that on a tyme as he walked with Johan Frauncis his nevewe in an orcharde at Farrare, in y⁰ talkynge of the love of Chryft he brake out in to thefe wordes, nevew, fayd he, this wyll I fhewe the, I warne the kepe it fecrete : the fubftaunce y' I have lefte after certayne bokes of myne finyfshed I entende to gyve out to pore folke, & fencynge my felfe with the crucifyx, bare fote walkynge about the worlde, in every towne and caftell I purpofe to preche of Chryft. Afterwarde I underftande by the efpecyall commaundement of God he chaunged that purpofe and appoynted to profeffe hym felfe in the ordre of freres prechours.

OF HIS DETH.

In y⁰ yere of our redempcion, M.CCCC.xCiiii. whan he had fulfylled y⁰ xxxii. yere of his age & abode at Florence, he was fodenly taken with a fervent axes ²² which fo ferforth crepte in to y⁰ interiori pertes of his body, y' hit dyfpyfed all medycynes & overcame all remedy, and compelled him within thre dayes to fatisfye nature and repaye her y⁰ lyfe whiche he receyved of her.

After that he hadde receyved the holy body of our Savyour whan they offred unto hym the crucyfyx (y' in the ymage of Chryftes ineffable paffion fuffred for oure fake he myght ere he gave up the ghoft receyve his full draught of love and compaffyon in the beholdynge of that pytefull figure as a ftronge defence agaynft all adverfyte and a fure port culioufe againft wikked fpirites) the preeft demaunded hym whether he fermly beleved y' crucyfyx to be the Image of hym that was very God & very man : whiche in his Godhed was before all time begoten of his father : to whome he is alfo equall in all thynge : and whiche of y° Holy Ghoft God alfo : of hym & of the Father coeternalli goynge forth (whiche .iij. per-fones be one God) was in y° chafte wombe of our lady a perpetuall virgyne conceyved in time : which fuffred hungre, thruft, hete, colde, laboure, travayle, & watche : and whiche at the lafte for wafshynge of our fpotty fynne contracted and drawen unto us in the fynne of Adame, for the foveraigne love that he had to mankynde, in the aulter of the croffe wyllyngely & gladly fhedde out his mooft precyoufe blode. When y° preeft enquyred of him thefe thynges & fuche other as they be wonte to enquere of folke in fuche cafe, Picus anfwered hym y' he not onely beleved hit but alfo certaynly knewe it. Whan y' one Albertus [23] his fyfters fone : a yonge man both of wit, connynge, & condicyons excellent : began to conforte hym agaynft deth : & by natural reafon to fhewe hym why hit was not to be fered but ftrongely to be taken : as y' onely thynge which maketh an ende of all y° laboure, payne, trouble, & forowe of this fhort miferable deedly

lyfe : he anfwered y' this was not the cheyefe thyng y'
fholde make hym content to dye : bycaufe y' deth de-
termyneth the manyfolde incommoditees and paynfull
wretchednes of this life : but rather this caufe fholde
make hym not content onely but alfo glad to dye : for
that deth maketh an ende of fynne : in as moche as he
trufted y' fhortnes of his lyfe fholde leve hym no fpace
to fynne and offende.   He afked alfo all his fervauntes
forgyvenes, yf he had ever before that daye offended ony
of them.   For whom he had provyded by his teftament viij.
yeres before, for fome of them mete and drynk, for fome
money, eche of them after theyr defervynge.   He fhewed
alfo to the above named Albertus & many other credible
perfons y' y' quene of heven came to hym y' nyght with
a mervayloufe fragrant odour refrefshynge all his membres
y' were brofed & frufshed [24] with that fever, & promyfed
him that he fhold not utterly dye.   He lay alwaye with
a plefaunt and a mery countenaunce, and in the verye
twytches and panges of deth he fpake as though he
behelde y' hevens opene.   And all y' came to hym &
faluted hym offerynge theyr fervyce with very lovyng
wordes he receyved, thanked, & kyffed.   The executour
of his moveable goodes he made one Antony his brother.[25]
The heyer of his landes he made y' pore people of the
hofpytall of Florence.   And in this wyfe in to y' handes
of oure Savyoure he gave up his fpiryte.

HOW HIS DETH WAS TAKEN.

What forowe and hevynes his departyng out of this
worlde was : both to ryche and pore, hygh & lowe : well
teftyfyeth the prynces of Italye, well wytneffeth the
citees & people, well recordeth the grete benygnyte and
fynguler curtefye of Charles kynge of Fraunce,[26] which as

he came to Florence, entendynge from thens to Rome and fo forth in his vyage agaynſt the Realme of Naples, herynge of the fykenes of Picus, in all convenyent haſte he fent hym two of his owne phiſicions as embaſſiatours both to viſet hym and to do hym all yᵉ helpe they myght : and over that fent unto hym letters fubfcribed with his owne hande full of fuche humanyte and courteyſe offres as the benevolent mynde of fuche a noble prince and the worthy vertues of Picus required.

OF THE STATE OF HIS SOULE.

After his deth (and not longe after) Hieronimus[27] a frere prechour of Ferrare, a man as well in connynge as holynes of lyvynge mooſt famous, in a fermone whiche he reherced in the cheyſe chyrche of all Florence fayd unto the people in this wyſe. O thou Cyte of Florence I have a fecrete thynge to ſhewe the which is as true as yᵉ gofpell of Saynt Johan. I wolde have kept hit fecrete but I am compelled to ſhewe hit. For he that hathe auctoryte to commaunde me, hath byd me publyſshe hit. I fuppoſe veryly that there be none of you but ye knewe Johan Picus Erle of Mirandula, a man in whom God had heped many grete gyftes and fynguler graces, yᵉ chyrche had of hym an ineſtymable loſſe, for I fuppoſe yf he myght have had the ſpace of his lyfe prorogyd : he ſholde have excelled (by fuche workes as he ſhold have lefte behynde hym) all them yᵗ dyed this .viii.C. yere before him. He was wonte to be converfaunt with me and to breke to me yᵉ fecretes of his herte : in whiche I perceyved that he was by privey infpyracion called of God unto relygion. Wherfore he purpofed oftentymes to obey this infpyra-cyon and folowe his callynge. Howbehit not beynge kynde ynoughe for fo grete benefices of God : or called bak by the tendernes of his flefshe (as he was a man of delicate complexion) he fhranke frome the laboure, or thinkynge happely y^t the religion had no nede of hym differred it for a tyme, howbehit this I fpeke onely by conjecture.[28] But for this delaye I thretened hym two yere togyther : y^t he wolde be punyfshed yf he for-flowthed that purpofe which our Lorde had put in his mynde, & certeynely I prayed to God my felfe (I wyll not lye therfore) that he myght be fom what beten : to compell hym to take that waye whiche God had from above fhewed hym. But I defyred not this fcourge upon hym y^t he was beten with : I loked not for that : but oure Lorde hadde fo decreed that he fholde forfake this prefent lyfe and leve a parte of that noble crowne that he fholde have had in heven. Notwithftondyng ye moft benygne juge hath dalt mercyfully with him : and for his plentyoufe almes gyven out with a free and liberall hande unto poore people & for the devout prayers whiche he mooft inftantly offred unto God this favoure he hath : though his foule be not yet in the bofome of oure Lorde in the hevenly joye : yet is hit not on y^t other fyde deputed unto perpetual payne, but he is adjuged for a whyle to the fyre of purgatory, there to fuffre payne for a feafon, which I am ye gladder to fhewe you in this by-halfe : to the entent y^t they which knewe hym : & fuche infpecially as for his manyfolde benyfyces are fingulerly beholden unto him : fholde now with theyr prayers, almes, & other fuffrages helpe hym. Thefe thynges this holy man Hierom, this fervaunt of God openly affermed, and alfo fayde that he knew wel if he lyed in that place : he were worthy eternall dampnacion. And over y^t he fayd y^t he had knowen all thofe thinges wythin a certain tyme, but ye wordes which Picus had fayde in his fykenes

27

of ye aperyng of our lady caufed him to doubt & to fere
left Picus had ben deceyved by fome illufyon of ye
devyll : in as moch as the promyfe of our lady femed to
have ben fruftrate by his dethe : but afterward he under-
ftode yt Picus was deceyved in the equivocacyon of ye
worde whyle fhe fpake of ye feconde deth & ever laftyng
& he undertoke her of ye fyrft deth & temporall.
And after this ye fame Hierom fhewed to his acquayn-
taunce yt Picus had after his deth apered unto him all
compaced in fire & fhewed unto him yt he was fuch wife
in purgatorye punyfhed for his neglygence & his un-
kyndnes. Now fyth hit is fo that he is adjuged to yt
fyre from which he fhal undoubtedly depart unto glory
& no man is fure how longe hit fhalbe fyrft : & may be
ye fhorter tyme for our interceffyons : let every chryften
body fhewe theyr charite upon hym to helpe to fpede
hym thyder where after the longe habitacion with ye in-
habytauntes of this derke worlde (to whom his goodly
converfacion gave grete lyght) & after ye darke fyre of
purgatory (in whiche venyall offences be clenfed) he may
fhortly (yf he be not all redy) entre ye inacceffible & infinite light of heven ; where he may in ye prefence of ye
foveraygne Godhed fo praye for us yt we may ye rather
by his interceffion be perteyners of yt infpecable joy
which we have prayed to bryng hym fpedely to. Amen.
Here endeth ye lyfe of Johan Picus Erle of Mirandula.

*Here foloweth thre epiftles of ye fayd Picus : of which thre
two be wryten unto Johan Fraunfces his nevew, the
thyrde unto one Andrewe Corneus
a noble man of Italy.*

Hit apereth by this epiftle y᷑ Johan Fraunfces the nevew of Picus had broken his mynde unto Picus and had made hym of counceyll in fome fecrete godly purpofe whiche he entended to take upon hym: but what this purpofe fholde be upon this lettre can we not fully perceyve. Nowe after y᷑ he thus entended, there fell unto hym many impedimentes & divers occafyons whiche withftode his entent and in maner letted hym & pulled hym bak, wherfore Picus comforteth hym in this epyftle and exorteth hym to perfeveraunce, by fuch meanes as are in the epyftle evydent and playne ynough. Notwithftondynge in yᵉ begynnyng of this lettre where he fayth that the flefhe fhall (but yf we take good hede) make us dronke in the cuppes of Cerces and myfshappe us in to the lykenes & fygure of bruyte beeftes : thofe wordes yf ye perceyve theym not be in this wyfe underftonden. There was fomtyme a woman called Circes whiche by enchaunte-mente as Vyrgyll maketh mencyon ufed with a drynke to turne as many men as receyved hit in to dyvers likenes & fygures of fondrye beeftes, fome in to lyones, fome in to beeres, fome in to fwyne, fome in to wolfes, which afterwarde walked ever tame aboute her houfe and wayted upon her in fuche ufe or fervyce as fhe lyft to put unto them. In lykewyfe the flefshe yf it make us dronke in yᵉ wyne of voluptuous pleafure or make the foule leve the noble ufe of his reafon & enclyne unto fenfualite and affeccions of yᵉ body : then the flefshe chaungeth us from the figure of reafonable men in the lykenes of unreafonable beeftes, and y᷑ dyverfly : after the convenience & fymylytude

betwene our fenfuall affeccyons and the brutyfshe pro-
prytees of fondry beeftes : as the proude harted man in
to a lyon, the irous in to a beere, the lecheroufe in to a
gote, the dronken gloten in to a fwyne, the ravenous
extorcyoner in to a wolfe, the falfe defceyvoure in to a
foxe, mokkynge gefter in to an ape. From which beeftly
fhappe may we never be reftored to our owne lykenes
agayn : unto the tyme we have caft up agayne the drynke
of the bodely affeccyons by which we were in to thefe
fygures enchaunted. Whan there cometh fomtyme a
monftrouse beeft to the towne we ronne and are glad to
paye fome money to have fyght therof, but I fere yf men
wolde loke upon them felfe advyfedly : they fholde fe a
more monftroufe beeft nerer home : for they fholde
perceyve themfelfe by ye wretched inclinacion to divers
beeftly paffyons chaunged in theyr foule not in to the fhap
of one but of many beeftes, y^t is to faye of all them whofe
brutyfh appetytes they folow. Let us then beware as
Picus councelleth us y^t we be not dronken in ye cuppes of
Cerces, y^t is to fay in ye fenfuall affeccions of ye flefsh,
left we deforme ye image of God in our foules, after whofe
image we be made, & make our felfe worfe then idolatres,
for yf he be odioufe to God whiche turneth ye image of a
beeft in to god : how moche is he more odious which
torneth the ymage of God in to a beeft.

JOHAN PICUS ERLE OF MIRANDULA TO
JOHAN FRAUNSCES HIS NEVEW BY HIS
BROTHER HELTH IN HYM THAT IS
VERY HELTH.

That thou haft had many evyll occafyons after thy
departynge which trouble the & ftonde agaynft the vertuoufe purpofe that thou haft taken there is no caufe my

fone why thou fholdeft eyther mervayle therof, be fory therfore, or drede hit, but rather how grete a wondre were this yf onely to ye amonge mortall men ye way laye open to heven with out fwet, as though y^t now at erft the difceytfull worlde & the curfed devyll fayled, & as thoughe thou were not yet in ye flefshe : which coveyteth agaynft the fpyrite : and which falfe flefsh (but yf we watche & loke wel to our felf) fhal make us dronke in ye cuppes of Circes & fo deforme us in to monftrous fhappes of brutyfsh & unreafonable beeftes.   Remembre alfo that of thefe evyll occafyons the holy apoftle faynt James fayth thou haft caufe to be glad, writynge in this wyfe.   Gaudete fratres quum in temptationes varias incideritis.   Be glad fayth he my brethren whan ye fall in dyvers temptacions, and not caufeles : for what hope is there of glorye yf there be none hope of victorye : or what place is there for victory where there is no batayl : he is called to the crowne & triumphe whiche is provoked to the conflyéte & namely to that conflyét : in which no man may be overcom againft his will, & in which we nede none other ftrength to vaynquyfsh but y^t we lyft our felfe to vaynquifsh.   Very happy is a chriften man fyth y^t ye victory is bothe put in his owne fre wyll : & the rewarde of the vyétory fhal be farre greter than we can eyther hope or wyfshe.   Tell me I pray ye my mooft dere fone if ther be ought in this life of all thofe thingis : ye delite wherof fo vexeth and toffith thefe erthly myndes.   Is ther I fay oni of thofe trifles : in ye geting of which a man muft not fuffre many labours many difpleafurs & many miferies or he get hit.   The marchaunt thinkith him felfe well ferved if after X yeres failing, after a m. incommoditees, after a m. jeopardyes of his lyfe he may at laft have a litle the more gadered to gyther.   Of the court & fervyce of this worlde there is

nothyng y' I nede to wryte unto the, the wretchednes wherof
the experience hit felfe hath taught the & dayly techeth.
In obtaynyng y⁰ favour of y⁰ prynces, in purchafynge the
frendfhyp of y⁰ company in ambicyoufe labour for offyces
& honoures what an hepe of hevynes there is : how
grete anguifsh : how moche befynes & trouble I may
rather lerne of the then teche y*, whiche holdyng my felf
content with my bokes & refte, of a chylde have lerned
to lyve within my degree & as moche as I maye dwellynge
with my felfe nothynge out of my felf labour for, or longe
for.   Now then thefe erthly thynges flyper, uncertayne,
vyle & commune alfo to us and bruyte beeft fwetynge &
pantynge we fhall unneth obtayne : and loke we than to
hevenly thynges & goodly (whiche neyther eye hath feen
nor ere hath herde nor herte hath thought) to be drawen
flumbry & flepyng magrey our teth : as though neyther
God myght reygne nor thofe hevenly citezyns lyve without
us.   Certaynely if this worldly felicite were goten to us
with ydelnes and eafe : than myght fome man that fhrynketh
frome labour rather chefe to ferve y⁰ worlde then God.
But now yf we be fo labored in the waye of fynne as
moche as in the way of God and moche more (wherof the
dampned wretches crye out : Laffati fumus in via iniqui-
tatis.   We be weryed in the waye of wyckednes) then
muft it nedes be a poynte of extreme madnes yf we had
not lever labour there where we go from labour to rewarde
then where we go from labour to payne.   I paffe over
how grete peace & felycite hit is to the mynde whan a
man hath nothinge that grudgeth his confcience nor is not
appaled with the fecrete twiche of ony prevye cryme. This
pleafure undoubtedly farre excelleth all y⁰ pleafurs y' in
this lyfe may be obteyned or defyred : what thyng is
there to be defyred amonge y⁰ delytes of this worlde :

which in yᵉ fekynge wery us, in yᵉ havynge blyndeth us, in yᵉ lefyng payneth us. Doubteſt thou my fone whether the myndes of wycked men be vexed or not with contynuall thought and torment : hit is yᵉ worde of God whiche neyther maye deceyve nor be deceyved. Cor impij quaſi mare fervens quod quiefcere non poteſt. The wycked mannes herte is lyke a ſtormy fee yᵗ maye not reſt, there is to hym nothynge fure, nothyng pefeable, but all thynge ferefull, all thinge forowfull, all thyng deedly. Shall we then envye thefe men : fhall we folow them : & forgetynge our owne countre heven, & our owne hevenly Father where we were free borne : fhall we wylfully make our felfe theyr bondemen : & with them wretchedly lyvyng more wretchedly dye : and at yᵉ laſt mooſt wretchedly in everlaſtyng fyre be punifshed. O the derke myndes of men. O the blynde hertes. Who feyth not more clere than lyght that all thefe thynges be (as they fey) truer than trueth hit felfe, & yet do we not that yᵗ we knowe is to be done. In vayne we wolde pluk our fote out of the clay but we ſtyk ſtyll. There fhall come to the my fone doubte hit not (in thefe places namely where thou art converfaunt) innumerable impedimentes every hour : which myght fere the frome the purpofe of good and vertuoufe lyvynge & (but yf thou be ware) fhall throwe the downe hedlynge. But amonge all thynges the very deedly peſtylence is this : to be converfaunt daye and nyght among them whofe lyfe is not onely on every fyde an alleƈtyve to fynne : but over that all fet in the expugnacion of vertue, under theyr capitayne the devyll, under the banayre of deth, under the ſtipende of hell, fightynge agaynſt heven, agaynſt our Lorde God and agaynſt his Chriſt. But crye thou therfore with yᵉ prophete. Dirumpamus vincula eorum & projiciamus a nobis iugum ipforum.

Let us breke the bandes of them and let us caſt of the yooke
of them. Theſe be they whom (as yᵉ glorioufe apoſtle Saynt
Paule feith) our Lorde hath delyvered in to the paffyons of
rebuke and to a reprovable fenfe to do thofe thynges that
are not convenyente, full of all iniquite, full of envye, man-
ſlaughter, contencion, gyle, & malice: backbiters, odioufe to
God, contumelioufe, proude, ſtately, fynders of evell thynges,
folyſshe, diffolute, without affeccion, without covenaunt, without mercy. Whiche whan they dayely fe the juſtice of God,
yet underſtonde they not yᵗ fuche as thefe thynges commytte
are worthy deth: not onely they yᵗ do fuche thynges: but
alfo they which confent to yᵉ doynge: wherfore my chylde
go thou never aboute to pleafe them whome vertue difpleafeth: but evermore let thefe wordes of yᵉ apoſtyll be
before thyn eyen. Oportet magis Deo placere quàm
hominibus. We muſt rather pleafe God then men. And
remembre thefe wordes of Saynt Paule alfo. Si hominibus
placerem, fervus Chriſti non effem. If I fholde pleafe men
I were not Chriſtes fervaunt. Let entre in to thyn herte
an holy pryde & have dyfdayne to take them for mayſters
of thy lyvynge whiche have more nede to take yᵉ for a
maiſter of theyrs. Hit were farre more femynge yᵗ they
fholde with yᵉ by good lyvynge begyn to be men then
thou fholdeſt with them by yᵉ levynge of thy good purpofe
fhamfully begyn to be a beſt. There holdeth me fomtyme by almyghty God as hit were even a fwone and an
infenfibilite for wondre when I begyn in my felfe: I wot
never whether I fhall fey: to remembre or to forowe, to
mervayle or to bewayle the apetytes of men, or yf I fhall
more playnly fpeke: yᵉ very madnes not to beleve the
gofpell whofe trouthe the blode of marters cryeth, yᵉ
voyce of apoſtles fowneth, miracles proveth, reafon con-
fermeth, yᵉ worlde teſtifyeth, yᵉ elementes fpeketh,

devylles confeffeth.   But a ferre greter madnes is hit yf
thou doubt not but that the gofpell is true: to lyve then as
though thou doubteft not but that hit were falfe.   For yf
thefe wordes of the wordes of the gofpell be true, that hit
is very harde for a riche man to entre the kyngedome of
heven why do we dayly then gape after the hepynge up of
riches.   And yf this be true that we fholde feke for the
glorye and prayfe not that cometh of men, but that cometh
of God, why do we then ever hange upon the jugement &
opinyon of men and no man rekketh whether God lyke
hym or not.   And yf we furely beleve y^t ones the tyme
fhall come in whiche our Lorde fhall faye, go ye curfed
people in to everlaftynge fyre, & agayne, come ye my
bleffed chyldren poffede ye the kyngdome y^t hath ben
prepared for you from ye fourmynge of the world, why is
there nothyng then y^t we leffe fere then hell, or y^t we leffe
hope for then the kyngedome of God.   What fhall we fay
elles but y^t there be many chryften men in name but fewe
in dede.   But thou my fone enforce thy felfe to entre
by the ftreyght gate y^t ledeth to heven & take no hede
what thynge many men do : but what thyng ye verey law
of nature, what thyng very reafon, what thynge our Lorde
hym felfe fheweth y^e to be done.   For neyther thy glory fhal
be leffe yf thou be happy with fewe nor thy payne more
eafy yf thou be wretched with many.   Thou shalt have .ii.
fpecyally effectuall remedyes agaynft ye worlde & the
devyll with whiche two as with .ii. whynges thou fhalt
out of this vale of miferye be lyfte up in heven, that is to
faye, almes dede & prayer.   What maye we do without the
helpe of God, or how fhall he helpe us yf he be not called
upon.
   But over that : certaynely he fhall not here the whan
thou calleft on hym yf thou here not fyrft ye pore man

whan he calleth upon y^e, and verely hit is accordynge that God fholde defpyfe the beynge a man whan thou beynge a man defpyfeft a man. For hit is wryten: in what mefure y^t ye mete, hit fhall be mete you agayne. And in an other place of ye gofpell hit is fayd: blyffed be mercyfull men for they fhall gete mercy. Whan I ftyre the to prayer I ftyre ye not to ye prayer whiche ftondeth in many wordes, but to that prayer whiche in ye fecrete chambre of the mynde, in the prevy clofet of ye foule with very affecte fpeketh to God, and in ye mooft lyghtfome darkenes of contemplacion not onely prefenteth the mynde to the Father: but alfo unieth hit with him by infpekable wayes which onely they knowe y^t have affayed. Nor I care not how longe or how fhort thy prayer be, but how effectuall, how ardente, and rather interrupted & broken betwene with fighes then drawen on length with a contynuall rowe & nombre of wordes. Yf thou love thyne helth, yf thou defyre to be fure from ye grennes [29] of ye devyll, from the ftormes of this worlde, frome th' awayte of thyn enemyes, yf thou long to be acceptable to God, yf thou coveyte to be happy at the laft : let no day paffe the but thou ones at the left wife prefent thy felfe to God by prayer, and fallyng downe before hym flat to ye grounde with an humble affecte of devout mynde, not frome ye extremyte of thy lippes but out of ye inwardnes of thyn herte, cry thefe wordes of ye prophete. Delicta juventutis mee & ignorantias meas ne memineris, fed fecundum mifericordiam tuam memento mei propter bonitatem tuam Domine. The offences of my youth and myn ignoraunces remembre not good Lorde, but after thy mercy Lorde for thy goodnes remembre me. Whan thou fhalt in thy prayer axe of God: both ye Holy Spyryte which prayeth for us & eke thyn owne neceffyte fhall every houre put in thy mynde, & alfo what thou fhalte praye for : thou fhall fynde mater ynough in y⁰ redynge of holy fcrypture which y¹ thou woldeft now (fettynge poetes fables & tryfles a fyde) take ever in thyn hand I hartly pray y⁰.³⁰ Thou mayft do nothynge more pleafaunte to God, nothynge more profitable to thy felfe : then yf thyn hande ceafe not day nor nyght to turne and rede the volumes of holy fcrypture. There lyeth pryvely in them a certayn hevenly ftrength quyk and effeᶜtual, wich with a merveylous power transfourmeth & chaungeth y⁰ reders mynde in to the love of God, yf they be clene and lowly entreated. But I have paffed nowe y⁰ boundes of a lettre, y⁰ mater drawynge me forth & the grete love y¹ I have had to the, bothe ever before : & fpecyally fyth y¹ houre in which I have had fyrft knowledge of thy mooft holy purpofe. Now to make an ende with this one thynge I warne y⁰ (of which whan we were laft togyther I often talked with y⁰) that thou never forget thefe. ii. thynges, y¹ both y⁰ Sone of God dyed for y⁰ & y¹ thou fhalt alfo thy felfe dye fhortly, lyve thou never fo longe. With thefe twayne as with two fpurres, y⁰ one of fere y⁰ other of love, fpurre forthe thyn hors through y⁰ fhorte way of this momentarye lyfe to y⁰ rewarde of eternall felicyte, fyth we neyther ought nor maye prefere our felfe onye other ende than the endles fruycion of y⁰ infinite goodnes bothe to foule & body in everlaftynge peace.

Fare well and fere God.³¹

This Andrewe a worfhypfull man and an efpeciall frende of Picus hadde by his lettres gyven hym counceyll to leve the ftudy of phylofophy, as a thynge in which he thought Picus to have fpent tyme ynough & whiche : but yf it were applyed to yᵉ ufe of fome actuall befines : he juged a thyng vayne & unprofytable : wherfore he coun- ceyled Pycus to furceace of ftudy and put hym felfe with fome of yᵉ grete prynces of Italy, with whome (as this Andrew fayd) he fholde be moche more fruytefully occupyed then alway in the ftudye & lernyng of philo- fophye, to whom Picus anfwered as in this prefent epeftle appereth. Where he fayth thefe wordes (By this hit fhold folowe yᵗ hit were eyther fervyle or at the left wyfe not pryncely to make yᵉ ftudy of phylofophy other then mercen- nari) thus he meaneth. Mercennary we cal all thofe thynges whiche we do for hyre or rewarde. Then he maketh philofophy mercennary & ufeth hit not as connynge but as marchaundyfe whiche ftudyeth hit not for pleafure of hit felfe : or for the inftruccyon of his mynde in mortall vertue : but to applye hit to fuche thynges where he may get fome lucre or worldly advauntage.

JOHAN PICUS ERLE OF MYRANDULA TO ANDREWE CORNEUS GRETYNGE.

Ye exhorte me by your letters to the cyvyle and actyve lyfe, fayenge yᵗ in vayne : and in maner to my rebuke & fhame : have I fo longe ftudyed in philofophy : but yf I wolde at the laft excercife yᵉ lernynge in yᵉ entretynge of fome profitable actes & outwarde byfynes. Certaynly my welbeloved Andrewe I had caft awaye bothe coft & laboure of my ftudy : yf I were fo mynded that I coude fynde in my herte in this mater to affent unto you & folowe your councell. This is a very deedly and mon- ftrous perfuacyon which hath entred the myndes of men : belevynge that yᵉ ftudyes of phylofophye are of eftates &

prynces : eyther utterly not to be touched : or at left wife
with extreme lyppes to be fypped: and rather to the pompe
& oftentacion of theyr wit then to the culture & profyte
of theyr myndes to be lytel & eafely tafted. The wordes
of Neoptolemus they holde utterly for a fure decree : that
phylofophy is to be ftudyed eyther never or not longe : [32]
but the fayenges of wyfe men they repute for japes &
very fables : that fure & ftedfaft felicite ftondeth onely in
the goodnes of the mynde, & that thefe outwarde thynges
of ye body or of fortune lytle or nought pertayne unto
us. But here ye wyll faye to me thus. I am contente ye
ftudye, but I wolde have you outwardly occupyed alfo.
And I defyre you not fo to embrace Martha that ye fholde
utterly forfake Mary. Love them & ufe them both, as
well ftudy as worldly occupacion. Trewly my welbeloved
frende in this poynt I gayne fey you not, they that fo do I
fynde no fault in nor I blame them not, but certaynly hit is
not all one to fey we do well yf we do fo : and to fey we do
evyll but yf we do fo. This is farre out of the way : to
think that from contemplacyon to the aftyfe lyving, that
is to fey from the better to the worfe, is none errour to
declyne : and to thynke that it were fhame to abyde
ftyll in the better and not declyne. Shall a man then be
rebuked by caufe that he defyryth and enfueth vertue
only for hit felfe : by caufe he ftudyeth ye myfteryes of
God : by caufe he enfercheth the counceyll of nature : by
caufe he ufeth continually this plefaunt eafe & reft :
fekynge none outwarde thyng, difpifing all other thynge :
syth thofe thynges are able fuffyciently to fatisfye y^e
defyre of theyr folowers. By this rekenynge hit is a
thynge eyther fervyle or at ye left wife not princely to
make ye ftudy of wyfdom other then mercennarye: who
may well here this, who may fuffre hit. Certaynly he

39

never ftudyed for wyfedome which fo ftudied therfore that in tyme to come eyther he myght not or wolde not ftudy therfore, this man rather excercifed yᵉ ftudy of marchaundyfe then of wyfedom. Ye wryte unto me that hit is tyme for me now to put my felfe in houfhoulde with fome of the grete prynces of Italy but I fe well yᵗ as yet ye have not knowen the opynion that phylofophres have of them felfe, which (as Horace fayth) repute them felfe kynges of kinges:³³ they love lyberte: they can not bere yᵉ proud maners of eftates : they can not ferve. They dwell with them felfe and be content with the tranquyllyte of theyr owne mynde, they fuffyce them felfe & more, they feke nothynge out of them felfe : yᵉ thynges that are had in honoure amonge yʳ commune people : amonge them be not holden honourable. All that ever the volup-tuoufe defyre of men thyrfteth for : or ambycyon fygheth for : they fet at nought & defpife. Which while hit belongeth to all men : yet undoubtedly it perteyneth mooft proprely to them whome fortune hath fo lyberally favoured that they may lyve not onely well and plenteoufly but alfo nobly. Thefe grete fortunes lyfte up a man hye and fett hym out to the fhewe : but oftentymes as a fyerfe and a fkyttyfsh hors they caft of theyr mayfter. Certeynly alway they greve and vexe hym and rather tere hym then bere hym. The golden mediocrite, the meane eftate is to be defyred whiche fhall bere us as hit were in handes³⁴ more eafeli : which fhall obey us & not mayftre us. I ther-fore abydyng fermely in this opynyon fet more by my litle houfe, my ftudy, the pleafure of my bokes, yᵉ reft and peace of my mynde : then by all your kynges palaces, all your commune befynes, all your glory, all the advauntage that ye hawke after and all the favoure of the court. Nor I loke not for this fruyte of my ftudy yᵗ I may therby

40

herafter be toſſed in the flode and rombelyng of your worldly beſyneſſe : but y^t I may ones bryng forth the chyldren that I travayle on : y^t I may gyve out ſome bokes of myn owne to the commune proffyte which may ſum what favour yf not of connyng yet at the leſt wyſe of wyt and dylygence. And by cauſe ye ſhall not thynk that my travayle & dyligence in ſtudy is ony thyng re-mytted or ſlakked : I gyve you knowledge y^t after grete fervent labour with moch watch and infatygable travayle I have lerned both the hebrew language and the chaldey, and now have I ſet hande to overcome the grete dyffyculte of the araby tonge. Theſe my dere frende be thynges whiche to apertaine to a noble prynce I have ever thought and yet thynke. Fare ye well. Wryten at Paris the .xv. daye of Octobre the yere of grace. M.CCCC.lxxxxii.[35]

THE ARGUMENT OF THE EPYSTLE FOLOWYNGE.

After that Johan Fraunſces ye nevew of Picus had (as hit apereth in ye fyrſt epiſtle of Picus to hym) begon a chaunge in his lyvynge : hit ſemeth by this lettre y^t the company of the court where he was converſaunt diverſly (as hit is theyr unmanerly maner) deſcanted therof to his rebuke as them thought : but as trueth was unto theyr owne. Some of them juged hit foly, ſome called hit hypocreſy, ſome ſcorned him, ſome ſclaundred hym, of all whiche de-meanour (as we maye of this epiſtle conjecture) he wrote unto this erle Picus his uncle, whiche in this lettre com-forted & encourageth him, as hit is in ye courſe therof evydent.

JOHAN PICUS ERLE OF MYRANDULA TO FRAUNSCES HIS NEVEW GRETYNGE IN OUR LORDE.

Happy art thou my fone whan that oure Lorde not onely gyveth the grace wel to lyve but alfo that whyle thou lyveft wel he gyveth ye grace to bere evyl wordes of evyll people for thy lyvynge well. Certaynly as grete a prayfe as hit is to be commended of them y^t are commendable, as grete a commendacion it is to be reproved of them y^t are reprovable. Notwithftondynge my fone I call the not therfor happy by caufe this fals reprofe is worfhypfull & gloryous unto the, but for bycaufe y^t our Lorde Jefu Chryft (which is not onely true but alfo trueth hit felfe) affermeth that oure rewarde fhall be plenteous in heven when men fpeke evyll to us & fpeke all evyll agaynft us lyvynge for his name.³⁶ This is an Apoftles dignyte : to be reputed dygne afore God to be defamed of wykked folke for his name. For we rede in the gofpell of Luke that the appoftles went joyfull and glad from ye counfeill houfe of the Jewes bycaufe God had accepted theym as worthy to fuffre wronge and repreffe for his fake. Let us therfore joye and be glad yf we be worthy fo grete worfhyp before God y^t his worfhyp be fhewed in our rebuke. And yf we fuffre of ye world ony thyng that is grevous or bytter : let this fwete voyce of our Lorde be our confolacion. Si mundus vos odio habet, fcitote quia priorem me vobis odio habuit. Yf the worlde (fayth our Lorde) hate you, knowe ye y^t hit hated me before you. If ye worlde then hated him by whome ye worlde was made : we mooft vyle & fimple men and worthy (yf we confydre our wreched lyvynge well) all fhame & reproufe : yf folke bakbyte us & faye evyll of us : fhall we fo grevoufly take hit y^t left they fhold fay evyll we fholde begyn to do evyll. Let us rather gladly receyve thefe evyl wordes, and yf we be not fo happy to fuffre for vertue & trueth ¯as the olde feyntes fuffred betynges, byndynges, pryfon, fwerdes, & deth : let us thynke at the left wife we be well ferved yf we have ye grace to fuffre chydynge, detraccion, & hatred of wikked men, left y^t yf all occafion of defervynge be taken awaye ther be lefte us none hope of rewarde. Yf men for thy good lyvynge prayfe the : thy vertue certaynly in y^t hit is vertue maketh the lyke unto Chryft : but in that hit is prayfed hit maketh the unlike him : which for the reward of his vertue receyved ye opprobryoufe deth of the croffe : for which as the apoftle fayth God hath exalted hym and gyven hym a name y^t is above all names. More defyre-full is than to be condempned of the worlde and exalted of God then to be exalted of the worlde and condempned of God : ye worlde condemneth to lyfe, God exalteth to glorye : ye worlde exalteth to a fall, God condempneth to ye fyre of hell. Fynaly yf ye worlde fawne upon y^e : unneth hit may be but y^t thy vertue (which all lyfte upwarde fholde have God alone to pleafe) fhall fomwhat unto ye blandifshynge of ye worlde & favoure of ye people inclyne. And fo thoughe hit lefe nothynge of y^e in-tegrite of our perfeccion : yet hit lefeth of the rewarde, which reward whyle hit begynneth to be payde in ye worlde where all thynge is lytle, hit fhal be leffe in heven where al thing is grete. O happy rebukes which make us fure : y^t neither ye floure of our vertue fhall wyther with the peftilent blaft of vaynglorye : nor our eternall rewarde be mynyfshed for the vayn promocion of a lytell populare fame. Let us my fone love thefe rebukes, & onely of ye ignomynye and reprefe of our Lordes croffe let us lyke feythfull fervauntes with an holy ambycyon be proude. We (fayth Saynt Paule) preche Chryft cruci-fyed, which is unto ye Jewes difpite, unto ye Gentyles foly, unto us ye vertue and wyfedom of God. The wyfdom of this worlde is folyfshnes afore God, & the foly of Chryft is y^t by which he hath overcome ye wyfedom of ye worlde : by whiche hit hath pleafed God to make his belivyng people fafe.

If that thou doubte not but y^t they be madde whiche bakbite thy vertue : which the chryften lyvynge y^t is very wifedom reputeth for madnes : confidre than how moche were thy madnes, yf thou fholdeft for the juge-ment of madde men fwarve frome the good inftitution of thy lyfe,.namely fith all errour is with amendement to be taken awaye & not with imitacion & folowynge to be encreafed. Let theym therfore nyghe, let theym bawl, let them barke, go thou boldely forth thy journey as thou haft begone, and of the wyckednes & myfery confidre how moche thy felfe arte beholden to God : whiche hath illumined ye fyttynge in the fhadowe of dethe, and tranf-latynge the out of the company of them (which lyke dronken men with out a guyde wandre hyther and thyther in obfcure derkenes) hath affociate the to the chyldren of lyght. Let that fame fwete voyce of our Lorde alwaye fowne in thyn eres. Sine mortuos fepelire mortuos fuos, tu me fequere. Let deed men alone with deed men, folowe thou me. Deed be they that lyve not to God, and in the fpace of this temporall dethe laboryoufly purchafe them felfe eternall deth. Of whom yf you axe wherto they drawe : wherto they referre theyr ftudyes, theyr werkes & theyr befynes, & fynally what ende they have appoynted them felfe in the adepcyon wherof they fholde be happy : eyther they fhall have utterly nothynge

44

to anfwere, or they fhall bryng forth wordes repugnaunt in them felf & contrary eche to other lyke the ravynge of bedelem people. Nor they wot never them felfe what they do, but lyke them that fwyme in fwyfte flodes they be borne forth with yᵉ violence of evyll cuftom as hit were with the boyftious courfe of yᵉ ftreme. And theyr wikkednes blyndynge them on this fyde : & the devyl prikkynge them forwarde on that fyde : they renne forthe hedlyng in to all mifchiefe, as blynde guydes of blynde men, tyll that dethe fet on them unware, & tyll that hit be fayd unto them that Chryft fayth in the gofpell, my frende this nyght yᵉ devylles fhall take thy foule from the : thefe goodes then that thou hafte gedered whofe fhall they be. Then fhall they envy them whom they defpifed. Then fhal they commend them that they mokked. Then fhall they coveyte to enfew them in lyvyng whan they may not : whom whan they myght have enfewed they purfewed. Stop therfore thyn eres my mooft dere fone, & what fo ever men fey of yᵉ, what fo ever men thynke on yᵉ, accompt hit for nothynge, but regarde onely yᵉ jugement of God, which fhall yelde every man after his owne werkes when he fhall fhewe hym felfe frome heven with yᵉ aungels of his vertue : in flame of fyre doynge vengeaunce upon them that have not knowen God nor obeyed his gofpell, wich (as the apoftle feyth) fhal fuffre in deth eternall peyn, from yᵉ face of our Lorde, & frome the glory of his vertue, whan he fhall come to be gloryed of his feyntes & to be made merveylous in all them yᵗ have beleved. Hit is wryten. Nolite timere qui corpus poffunt occidere, fed qui animam poteft mittere in gehennam. Fere not them (feyth our Lorde) that may fle the body : but fere hym yᵗ may caft the foule in to helle. How moche leffe then be they to be fered : yᵗ

may neyther hurt foule nor body : which yf they now bakbyte y⁰ lyvynge vertuoufly, they fhall do the fame never the
leffe : yf (vertue forfaken) thou were over whelmed with
vyce : not for yᵗ vyce difpleafeth them but for yᵗ y⁰ vyce
of bakbytynge alway pleafeth them. Flee yf thou love
thyn helth, flee as ferre as thou mayft theyr companye,
and retournynge to thy felfe oftentymes fecretly pray
unto y⁰ mooft benygne father of heven, cryenge with the
prophete. Ad Te Domine levaui animam meam : Deus
meus in Te confido, non erubefcam, etiam fi irrideant me
inimici mei. Etenim univerfi qui fperant in Te non confundentur. Confundantur iniqua agentes fupervacue.
Vias tuas Domine demonftra mihi, et femitas tuas edoce
me. Dirige me in veritate tua, et doce me : quia Tu es
Deus Salvator meus, et in Te fperabo tota die.³⁷ That is to
faye. To Y⁰ Lorde I lyfte up my foule : in The I truft, I fhall
not be fhamed, & thoughe myne enemies mok me. Certaynly all they yᵗ truft in The fhall not be a fhamed. Let
them be a fhamed that worke wyckednes in vayne. Thy
weyes good Lorde fhewe me, and thy pathes teche me.
Directe me in thy trueth, and teche me : for thou arte God
my Savyoure, in The fhall I truft all the daye. Remembre
alfo my fone yᵗ the dethe lyeth at hande. Remembre
that all the tyme of our lyfe is but a moment & yet leffe
than a moment. Remembre how curfed our olde enemy
is : whiche offereth us y⁰ kyngdomes of this world that he
myght beryve us y⁰ kyngdome of heven : how falfe the
flefshly plefures : which therefore embrace us yᵗ they
might ftrangle us : how difceyteful thefe worldly
honoures : which therfore lyfte us up : yᵗ they myght
throwe us downe : how deedly these rycheffes : whiche
the more they fede us, y⁰ more they poyfon us : how
fhorte, how uncertayne, how fhadowe like falfe ymaginary

46

hit is y' all thefe thynges togyther may brynge us : & though they flowe to us as we wolde wyfsh them. Remembre agayne how grete thynges be promyfed and prepared for them : which difpifynge thefe prefent thynges defire and longe for that countre whofe kynge is y" God-heed, whofe law is charite, whofe mefure is eternite. Occupi thy mynde with thefe meditacyons and fuche other y' may waken the when thou flepeft, kyndle y" when thou waxes colde, conferme the when thou wavereft, & exhibit y" whynges of the love of God whyle thou laboreft to hevenwarde, that whan thou comeft home to us (which with grete defyre we loke for) we may fe not onely hym that we coveyte but alfo fuche a maner one as we coveyte. Fare well and love God whom of olde thou haft begon to fere. At Ferare the. ii. day of July the yere of our redempcion. M.CCCC.lxxxxii.

THE INTERPRETACION OF JOHAN PICUS UPON THIS PSALME CONSERVA ME DOMINE.[38]

Conferva me Domine quoniam fperavi in Te. Dixi Domino : Deus meus es Tu, quoniam bonorum meorum non eges. Sanćtis qui funt in terra mirificavit voluntates fuas. Multiplicate funt infirmitates eorum poftea accele-raverunt. Non congregabo conventicula eorum de fan-guinibus : nec memor ero nominum eorum per labia mea. Dominus pars hereditatis mee & calicis mei : Tu es qui reftitues hereditatem meam mihi. Funes ceciderunt mihi in preclaris : etenim hereditas mea preclara eft mihi. Benedicam Dominum qui tribuit mihi intellećtum : et vfque ad noćtem increpuerunt me renes mei. Providebam Deum in confpećtu meo femper, quoniam a dextris eft mihi ne commovear. Propter hoc letatum eft cor meum et exultavit lingua mea infuper et caro mea requiefcet in fpe. Quia non derelinques animam meam in inferno : nec dabis fanctum tuum videre corruptionem. Notas mihi fecifti vias vite : adimplebis me letitia cum vultu tuo. Delectationes in dextera tua vfque in finem.

Conferva me Domine. Kepe me good Lorde. If ony perfyte man loke upon his owne eftate there is one parell therin, y^t is to wyte, left he wax proude of his vertue, and therfore Davyd fpekyng in ye perfon of a ryghteous man of his eftate begynneth with thefe wordes. Conferva me Domine. That is to faye, kepe me good Lorde : whiche worde kepe me : yf it be well confydered : taketh awaye all occafyon of pryde. For he that is able of hym felf ony thynge to gete is able of him felf that fame thynge to kepe. He that afketh then of God to be kepte in the ftate of vertue fignifyeth in that afkynge that from the begynnynge he gote not that vertue by hym felfe. He then whiche remembreth y^t he attayned his vertue : not by his owne power but by the power of God : may not be proude therof but rather humbled before God after thofe wordes of th apoftle. Quid habes quod non accepifti. What haft thou that thou haft not receyved. And yf thou haft receyved hit : why arte thou proude therof as though thou haddeft not receyved it. Two wordes then be there which we fholde ever have in our mouthe : ye one. Miferere mei Deus. Have mercy on me Lorde : whan we remembre our vyce : that other. Conferva me Deus. Kepe me good Lorde : when we remembre our vertue.

Quoniam fperavi in Te. For I have trufted in Y^e. This one thynge is it that maketh us obtayne of God oure petycion, y^t is to wyte, whan we have a full hope & truft that we fhall fpede. Yf we obferve thefe two thynges in our requeſtes, yᵗ is to wyte, yᵗ we requyre nothynge but that whiche is good for us and yᵗ we requyre hit ardently with a ſure hope that God ſhall here us, our prayers ſhall never be voide. Wherfore whan we miſſe the effecte of our petycyon, eyther hit is for yᵗ we aſke ſuch thynge as is noyous unto us, for (as Chriſt ſayth) we wot never what we aſke, and Jeſus ſayd what ſo ever ye ſhall aſke in my name hit ſhall be gyven you (this name Jeſus ſignifyeth a ſavyour, and therfore there is nothynge aſked in yᵉ name of Jeſus but that is holſome and helpyng to the ſalvacion of the aſker) or elles God hereth not oure prayoure by-cauſe that thoughe yᵉ thynge yᵗ we requyre be good yet we aſke hit not well, for we aſke hit with lytle hope. And he yᵗ aſketh doubtyngely aſketh coldely & therfore Saynt James biddeth us aſke in ſayth nothyng doubtyng.

Dixi Domino : Deus meus es Tu. I have ſayd to our Lorde : my God arte Thou. After that he hath warded & fenced him ſelfe agaynſt pryd he deſcrybeth in theſe wordes his eſtate. All the eſtate of a ryghteous man ſtandeth in theſe wordes. Dixi Domino : Deus meus es Tu. I have ſayd to oure Lorde : ·my God arte Thou. Whiche wordes though they ſeme commune to all folke, yet are there very few yᵗ may ſaye them truely. That thyng a man taketh for his god that he taketh for his chyefe good. And that thynge taketh he for his chyefe good which onely had, though all other thynges lak, he thynketh hym ſelfe happy, & whiche onely lakyng, though he have al other thynges, he thinketh him ſelf unhappy. The negard then ſeyth to his money : deus meus es tu, my god art thou. For though honour fayle & helth and ſtrenghte and frendes, ſo he have money he thynketh him ſelfe well. And yf he have al thoſe thinges yᵗ we have ſpoken of, yf money fayle he thinketh him ſelfe unhappy. The gloton

feyth unto his flefshly luft, yᵉ ambycioufe man feyth to his
vaynglory: my god art thou. Se than how few may
trewly fey thefe wordes, I have fayde to oure Lorde : my
God arte Thou. For onely he maye trewly faye it whiche
is content with God alone : fo yᵗ yf there were offred hym
all the kyngdomes of the worlde and all the good that is
in erth and all the good that is in heven, he wolde not
ones offende God to have them all. In thefe wordes
than, I have feyd to our Lord : my God art Thou, ftandeth
all the ftate of a ryght wyfe man.

Quoniam bonorum meorum non eges. For thou haft
no nede of my good. In thefe wordes he fheweth yᵉ caufe
why he fayth onely to our Lorde : Deus meus es tu, my
God art Thou. The caufe is for that onely oure Lorde
hath no nede of oure good. There is no creature but yᵗ
it nedeth other creatures, and though they be of leffe
perfeccyon than hit felfe, as phylofophers and divynes
proven : for yf thefe more imperfyte creatures were not,
yᵉ other that are more parfyte coude not be. For yf ony
parte of yᵉ hole unyverfyte of creatures were diftroyed
& fallen to nought all the hole were fubverted. For certaynly one part of that univerfyte perifshyng all parties
perifsh, and all creatures be partis of yᵗ univerfyte, of which
univerfyte God is no parte, but he is the begynnyng
nothyng there upon dependynge. For nothynge truely
wanne he by yᵉ creacyon of this worlde, nor nothynge
fholde he lefe yf the worlde were adnychylate and
turned to nought agayn. Than onely God is he whiche
hath no nede of oure good. Well ought we certaynly
to be a fhamed to take fuche thynge for god as hath
nede of us, & fuche is every creature. Moreover we
fhold not accept for god, yᵗ is to faye for the chyefe
goodnes, but onely yᵗ thynge whiche is the mooft

50

foverayne goodnes of all thynges, and that is not the goodnes of ony creature, onely therfore to our Lorde ought we to faye : my God art Thou.

Sanctis qui funt in terra ejus mirificavit voluntates fuas. To his fayntes that are in yᵉ londe of hym he hath made mervelous his willes. After God fholde we fpecially love them which are nereft joyned unto God, as be the holy aungelles & blyffed fayntes that are in theyr countree of heven : therfore after that he had fayd to oure Lorde : my God arte thou : he addeth ther-unto that oure Lorde hathe made mervelous his wylles, yᵗ is to faye he hathe made mervelous his loves and his defyres towarde his feyntes that are in the londe of hym, that is to wyte, in the countree of heven whiche is called yᵉ londe of God and the londe of lyvynge people. And veryly yf we inwardly confydre how grete is the felicite of that countree & how moche is yᵉ mifery of this worlde, how grete is yᵉ goodnes and charyte of thofe bleffed citezyns : we fhall continually defyre to be hens that we were there. Thefe thynges & fuch other whan we remembre, we fhold ever more take hede yᵗ our medi-tacions be not unfruytfull, but that of every meditacyon we fhold alwayes purchase one vertue or other, as for enfample by this meditacyon of the goodnes of that hevenly countree we fholde wynne this vertue that we fholde not onely ftrongly fuffre deth and pacyently whan our tyme cometh or yf hit were put unto us for yᵉ faith of Chryft : but alfo we fholde wyllyngely and gladly longe therfore, defyrynge to be departed out of this vale of wretchydnes yᵗ we may reygne in yᵗ hevenly countree with God & his holy fayntes.

Multiplicate funt infirmitates eorum poftea accelera-verunt. Theyr infyrmytees be multyplyed and after

51

they hafted.   Thefe wordes the prophete fpeketh of
wycked men.   By infyrmytees he underftondeth idoles
and fo hit is in yᵉ hebrew text.   For as good folke
have but one God whom they worfhyp, fo evyll folke
have many goddes and idoles, for they have many voluptuoufe pleafures many vayne defyres many dyvers paffyons whiche they ferve, & wherfore feke they many
fondry pleafures ? certainly for bycaufe they can fynde
none yᵗ can fet theyr herte at reft & for yᵗ (as yᵉ prophete fayth) wycked men walk about in a circuet or
compace wherof there is none ende.   Now after thefe
wordes : theyr Idoles be multiplied : hit foloweth.   After
they hafted : yᵗ is to fay : after theyr Idoles, after theyr
paffyons and beeftly defyres they ronne forth hedlynge un-
advyfedly without ony confideracyon.   And in this be we
taught that we fholde as fpedely ronne to vertue as they
ronne to vyce, & yᵗ we fhold with no leffe dylygence
ferve our Lorde God than they ferve theyr lorde yᵉ devyll.
The juft man confyderyng yᵉ eftate of evyll folke de-
termineth fermly with hym felfe (as we fholde alfo)
that utterly he wyll in no wyfe folowe them, & therfore he faith.   Non congregabo conventicula eorum de
fanguinibus : nec memor ero nominum.   I fhall not gather
the congregacyon of them frome the blode : nor I fhall not
remembre theyr names, he fayth, from the blode : both
bycaufe Idolatres were wont to gather the blode of theyr
facrefyce togyther and theraboute to do theyr ferymonyes :
and alfo for that all the lyfes of evyll men forfaken reafon
whiche ftondeth all in the foule, and folowen fenfualyte
that ftondeth all in yᵉ blode, the prophete faith not onely
that he wyll not gather theyr congregacyon togyther from
yᵉ blode, that is to fay yᵗ he wolde do no facrefyce to thofe
idoles but alfo that he wolde not remembre theyr names,

that is to fay that he wolde not talke nor fpeke of y^e
voluptuoufe delytes whiche are evyll peoples goddes,
which we myght yet lawfully do : fhewynge us by y^t :
that a parfyte man fholde abftayne not onely from unlawfull
pleafures but alfo frome lawfull, to th'ende y^t he may all
togyther hole have his mynde in to hevenwarde and the
more purely entende unto the contemplacion of hevenly
thynges. And for as moche as fome man wolde peradventure thynke y^t hit were foly for a man utterly to de-
pryve him felfe from all pleafures, therfor ye prophete
addeth. Dominus pars hereditatis mee. Our Lorde is
ye part of myn enheretaunce. As though he wolde faye.
Mervayle the not though I forfake all thynge to th'entent
y^t I may have ye poffeffyon of God in whom all other
thynges alfo be poffeffed. This fhold be the voyce of
every good chryften man. Dominus pars hereditatis mee.
God is the parte of myne enheretaunce. For certaynly
we chryften people to whom God is promyfed for an
enheretaunce ought to be a fhamed to defyre ony thyng
befyde hym. But for y^t fome man myght happely repute
hit for a grete prefumpcion y^t a man fholde promyfe
hymfelfe God for his enherytaunce, therfore ye prophete
putteth therto. Tu es qui reftitues hereditatem meam
michi. Thou good Lorde arte he that fhall reftore myne
enherytaunce unto me. As though he wolde faye. O
good Lorde my God I know well that I am nothynge in
refpeét of Y^e, I wote well I am unable to affende by myne
owne ftrength fo hyghe to have Y^e in poffeffyon, but Thou
arte he y^t fhalt drawe me to the by thy grace, Thou arte he
that fhalte gyve thy felfe in poffeffion unto me. Let a
ryghteous man then confydre how grete a felicite hit is to
have God fall unto hym as his enherytaunce : hit foloweth
in the pfalme. Funes ceciderunt mihi in preclaris. The

cordes have fallen to me nobly. The partes and lottes of enherytaunces were of olde tyme met out and dyvyded by cordes or ropes. Thefe wordes then, the ropes or cordes have fallen to me nobly, be as moche to fay as the parte or lot of myne enherytaunce is noble. But for as moche as there be many men which though they be called to this grete felycite (as indede all chriften people are) yet they fet lytel thereby and often tymes chaunge hit for a fmall fymple delyte, therfore yᵉ prophete faith fuyngly. Hereditas mea preclara eft michi. Myn enheritaunce is noble to me. As though he wolde fay that as hit is noble in hit felfe fo hit is noble to me, that is to faye I reputed hit noble, and all other thynges in refpecte of hit I repute (as Saynt Paule fayth) for donge. But for as moche as to have this lyght of underftandynge whereby a man may know this gyft that is gyven hym of God to be the gyft of God, therfore the prophete fuyngely fayth. Benedicam Dominum, qui tribuit intellectum. That is to faye. I fhall blyffe our Lorde which hath gyven me underftondinge. But in fo moche as a man oftentymes entendeth after reafon to ferve God, and yᵗ notwithftondyng yet fenfualite and the flefsh repugneth : than is a man perfyte whan yᵗ not his foule onely but alfo his flefsh drawe forthe to Godwarde after thofe wordes of the prophete in an other pfalme. Cor meum & caro mea exultaverunt in Deum vivum. That is to faye. My mynde & my flefshe both have joyed in to livynge God. And for this the prophete fayth here fuyngely. Et ufque ad noctem increpuerunt me renes mei. My reynes or kidney hath chyden me unto the nyght. That is to faye. My reynes, in which is wont to be the greteft inclinacyon to concupifcence, not onely nowe enclyne me not to fynne but alfo chydeth me, that is to fay, withdrawe me from fynne unto the nyght, that is to faye, they ſo ferforth withdraw me from ſynne that wyllyngly they afflyꝗt and payne my body.   Afflyccyon is in ſcrypture oftentymes ſignified by the nyght bycauſe hit is the mooſt dyſcomfortable ſeaſon.   Then ſuyngly the prophete ſheweth what is yᵉ rote of this privacion or takynge awaye of fleſshly concupiſcence in a man, ſayenge.   Providebam Deum in conſpeꝗtu meo ſemper.   I provyded God alway before me ſight.   For yf a man had God alwaye before his eyen as a ruler of all his werkes, & in all his werkes he ſholde neyther ſeke his owne lucre his gloryе nor his owne pleaſure but onely to yᵉ pleaſure of God, he ſhold ſhortly be perfyte.   And for as moche as he yᵗ ſo dooth proſpereth in al thynge, therfore it foloweth.   Ipſe a dextris eſt mihi ne commovear.   He is on my ryght hand that I be not moved or troubled.   Then the prophete declareth how grete is yᵉ felycite of a juſt man, whiche ſhall be everlaſtyngly blyſſed bothe in body and in ſoule, and therfore he ſayth.   Letatum eſt cor meum.   My ſoule is glad knowyng yᵗ after deth heven is made redy for hym.   Et caro mea requieſcet in ſpe.   And my fleſshe ſhall reſt in hope.   That is to ſaye that thoughe it joye not by and by as in receyvynge his gloryous eſtate medyatly after the deth,[39] yet hit reſteth in the ſepulcre with this hope that it ſhall aryſe in the daye of judgemente immortall and ſhynynge with his ſoule.   And alſo the prophete more expreſſely declareth in the verſe folowing.   For where he ſayd thus, my ſoule is glad, he addeth the cauſe, ſayenge.   Quia non derelinques animam meam in inferno.   For thou ſhalt not leve my ſoule in hell.   Alſo where the prophete ſayd that his fleſsh ſholde reſt in hope he ſheweth the cauſe, ſayeng.   Nec dabis ſanꝗtum tuum videre corruptionem.   Nor thou ſhalte not ſuffre thy ſaynt to ſe corrupcyon, that is to ſaye, thou ſhalte not ſuffre yᵉ fleſshe of a good man to be cor-

55

rupted. For that that was corruptyble fhall aryfe incor-
ruptible. And for as moche as Chryft was the fyrft whiche
entred paradife and opened the lyfe unto us, and was the
fyrft that rofe agayne and the caufe of our refurreccyon :
therefore thefe wordes that we have fpoken of the refurreccyon ben pryncipally underftonden of Chrift, as Saynt
Peter y⁰ apoftle hath declared, & fecondaryly they may be
underftonden of us in yᵗ we be the membres of Chrift,
which onely never fawe corrupcyon, for his holy body
was in his fepulcre nothyng putrified. For as moche
then as y⁰ way of good lyvyng bryngeth us to a perpetuall
lyfe of foule & body, therfore y⁰ prophete fayth. Notas
mihi fecifti vias vite. Thou haft made the wayes of lyfe
knowen unto me. And bycaufe that all the felycite
of that ftondeth in the clere beholdynge and fruycion of
God, therfore hit foloweth. Adimplebis me letitia cum
vultu tuo. Thou fhalt fyll me full of gladnes with thy
chere. And for that our felicite fhall be everlaftynge, therfore he fayth. Delectationes in dextra tua ufque in finem.
Delectacion & joy fhall be on thy ryght hande for ever :
he fayth on thy ryght hand bycaufe yᵗ our felycite is
fulfylled in the vyfyon and fruytion of the humanyte of
Chryft which fytteth in heven on y⁰ ryght hande of his
father's majefte, after y⁰ wordes of Saint Johan. Hec eft
tota merces, vt videamus Deum, & quem mififti Jefum
Chriftum. That is all oure rewarde that we maye beholde
God and Jefus Chryft whome thou haft fent : to whiche
rewarde he brynge us that fytteth there and prayeth for
us. Amen.

HERE BEGYN .XII. RULES OF JOHAN PICUS ERLE OF MYRANDULA PARTELY EXCYTYNG PARTELY DYRECTYNGE A MAN IN SPYRYTUALL BATAYLE.[40]

Who fo to vertue eftemeth the waye
Bycaufe we muft have warre contynuall
Agaynft ye worlde, ye flefsh, ye devyll, that aye
Enforce them felfe to make us bonde & thrall,
Let hym remembre that chefe what way he fhall
Even after the worlde, yet muft he nede fufteyn
Sorow, adverfite, labour, greyfe, and payne.

THE SECONDE RULE.

Thynke in this wretched worldes befy woo
The batayll more fharpe & lenger is I wys
With more laboure and leffe fruyte alfo
In whiche the ende of laboure labour is :
And when the worlde hath left us after this
Voyde of all vertue : the rewarde when we dye
Is nought but fyre and payne perpetually.

THE THYRDE RULE.

Confydre well that foly it is and vayne
To loke for heven with pleafure and delyght.
Sith Chryft our Lorde and fovereyne captayne
Afcended never but by manly fyght
And bytter paffion, then were it no ryght
That ony fervaunt, ye wyll your felfe recorde,
Sholde ftonde in better condicyon than his lorde.

THE FOURTH RULE.

Thynke how that we not onely fholde not grudge
But eke be glad and joyfull of this fyght,
And longe therfore all though we coude not judge
How that therby redounde unto us myght
Ony profyte, but onely for delyght
To be confourmed and lyke in fome behavour
To Jefu Chryft our bleffed Lorde & Savyoure.

As often as thou doft warre and ftryve,
By the refyftence of ony fynfull mocyon,
Agaynft ony of thy fenfuall wyttes fyve,
Caft in thy minde as oft with good devocyon
How thou refembleft Chryft : as with fowre pocyon
If thou payne thy taft : remembre therewithall
How Chryft for the tafted eyfell[41] and gall.

Yf thou withdrawe thyn handes and forbere
The raven of ony thynge : remembre than
How his innocent handes nayled were.
Yf thou be tempte with pryde : thynke how that whan
He was in forme of God : yet of a bonde man
He toke the fhap and humbled hym felfe for the
To the mooft odioufe and vyle deth of a tree.

Confydre when thou arte moved to be wrothe
He who that was God, and of all men the beft,
Seynge hym felfe fcorned, fcorged both,
And as a thefe betwene .ii. theves threft
With all rebuke and fhame : yet from his breft
Came never figne of wrath or of difdayne,
But pacyently endured all the payne.

Thus every fnare and engyne of the devyll
Yf thou this wyfe perufe them by and by:
There can be none fo curfed or fo evyll
But to fome vertue thou mayft it applye.
For ofte thou fhalt: refyftyng valyauntly
The fendes myght and fotle fyery darte:
Our Savyour Cryft refemble in fome parte.

THE FYFT RULE.

Remembre well that we in no wyfe muft
Neyther in the forefayd efpyrytuell armoure
Nor ony other remedy put our truft,
But onely in the vertue ftrength of our Savyour:
For he it is by whofe myghty powre
The worlde was veynquyfshed & his prynce caft out:
Whiche reygned before in all the erthe about. ·

In hym let us truft to overcome all evyll,
In hym let us put our hope and confydence,
To fubdewe the flefshe and mafter ye devyll,
To hym be all honour and lowly reverence:
Oft fholde we requyre with all our dylygence
With prayer, with teeres, & lamentable playntes
The ayde of his grace and his holy fayntes.

THE SYXTE RULE.

One fynne vaynquyfshed loke thou not tarye,
But lye in awayte for another every houre,
For as a wood[42] lyon the fende our adverfarye
Rynneth aboute fekynge whom he may devoure:
Wherfore contynually upon thy towre,
Left he the unpurveyed and unredy catche,
Thou muft with the prophete ftonde & kepe watche.

THE .VII. RULE.

Enforce thy felfe not onely for to ftonde
Unvaynquyfshed agaynft the devyls myght,
But over that take valyauntly on hande
To vaynquyfshe hym and put hym unto flyght :
And that is whan of yᵉ fame dede thought or fyght
By whych he wolde have the with fynne contract
Thou takeft occafyon of fome good vertuoufe acte.

Some tyme he fecretly caftyth in thy mynde
Some lawdable dede to ftere the to to pryde,
As vayn glorye makyth many a man blynde.
But let humylite be thy fure guyde,
Thy good wark to God let hit be applyede,
Thynke hit not thyn but a gyft of his
Of whofe grace undowtedly all goodnes is.

THE .VIII. RULE.

The tyme of batayle fo put thy felfe in preace⁴³
As though thou fhuldeft after that victorye
Enjoye for ever a perpetuall peace :
For God of his goodnes and lyberall mercy
Maye graunt the gyfte, & eke thy proude enemy,
Confounded and rebuked by thy batayle,
Shall the no more happely for very fhame affayle.

But when thou mayft ones yᵉ triumphe obtayne
Prepare thy felfe and trymme the in thy gere
As thou fholdeft incontinent fight agayn,
For yf thou be redy the devyll wyll the fere :
Wherfore in ony wyfe fo ever thou the bere

That thou remembre and have ever in memory
In victory batayle in batayle victory.

THE .IX. RULE.

If thou thynke thy felfe well fenced and fure
Agaynft every fotell fuggeftion of vyce,
Confydre frayle glaffe may no dyftres endure,
And grete adventurers ofte curs the dyce :
Jeopard not to farre therfore and ye be wyfe,
But evermore efchewe the occafyons of fynne,
For he that loveth parell fhall perefsh therin.

THE .X. RULE.

In all temptacyon withftonde the begynnynge :
The curfed infantes of wretched Babilon [44]
To fuffre them wax is a jeoperdous thynge :
Bete out theyr braynes therfore at the Stone :
Perylous is the canker that catcheth the bone :
To late cometh the medicine yf thou let the fore
By longe contynuaunce encreafe more & more.

THE .XI. RULE.

Though in the tyme of the batayle and warre
The conflecte feme bytter fharpe and fowre,
Yet confydre hit is more pleafure farre
Over the devyll to be a conqueroure
Then is in the ufe of thy beeftly pleafoure :
Of vertue more joye the confcience hath within
Then outwarde the body of all his fylthy fynne.

In this poynt many men erre for necligence,
For they compare not the joye of the vyctory
To the fenfuall pleafure of theyr concupifcence,

But lyke rude beeſtes unadviſedly
Lakkynge diſcrecyon they compare & applye
Of theyr fowle ſynne the voluptuouſe delyght
To the laberous travayle of the conflyct & fyght.

And yet alas he that ofte hath knowen
What gryefe it is by longe experyence
Of his cruell enemye to be over throwen,
Sholde ones at the leſt wyſe do his diligence
To prove and aſſaye with manly defence
What pleaſure there is, what honour peace & reſt
In glorioufe victorye tryumphe and conqueſt.

THE .XII. RULE.

Though thou be tempted diſpayre the nothynge :
Remembre the gloryous apoſtle Saynt Paule
Whan he had ſeen God in his perfyte beynge,
Leſt ſuche revelacyon ſholde his herte extolle,
His fleſshe was ſuffred rebell agaynſt the ſoule :
This dyd almyghty God of his goodnes provide
To preſerve his ſervaunt fro yᵉ daunger of pryde.

And here take hede that he whom God dyd love,
And for his mooſt eſpeciall veſſell choſe,
Ravyſshed into the thyrde heven above,
Yet ſtode in peryll leſt pryde myght hym depoſe :
Well ought we then our hertes fence & cloſe
Agaynſt vaynglorye the mother of repryeſe,
The very crop and rote of all myſchefe.

Agaynſt this pompe & wretched worldes gloſe
Conſydre how Criſt the Lorde, ſovereyne powere,
Humbled him ſelfe for us unto the croſſe :

And peradventure deth with in one houre
Shal us bereve welth ryches and honowre :
And bryng us down ful low both fmal & grete
To vyle caryon and wretched wormes mete.

Here folowe the .XII. wepens of fpirytual batayle
which every man fhuld have at hand when yᵉ plefure of
a fynful temptacyon commeth to his mynde.

The plefure lytle & fhort.

The folowers gryef &
hevynes.

The loffe of a bettyr thyng.

This lyfe a dreame and a
fhadowe.

The deth at our hand &
unware.

Yᵉ fere of impenitent de-
partyng.

Eternal joy eternal payne.

Ye nature & dygnyte of
man.

Yᵉ peace of a good mynde.

The grete benfytes of God.

The peynful cros of Cryft.

The wytnes of martyrs
and example of fayntes.

THE .XII. WEPENS HAVE WE[45] MORE AT LENGTH DECLARED AS HIT FOLOWYTH.

THE PLEASURE LYTLE AND SHORT.

Confydre well the pleafure that thou haft,
Stande hit in towchyng or in wanton fyght,
In vayne fmell or in thy lycoroufe taft,
Or fynally in what fo ever delyght
Occupyed is thy wretched appetyght :
Thou fhalt hit fynde when thou haft al caft
Lytle, fymple, fhort, and fodenly paft.

THE FOLOWERS GRYEFE & HEVYNES.

Ony good wark yf thou with labour do,
The labour goth, the goodnes doth remayne :
If thou do evyl with pleafure joyned therto,

63

The pleafure which thyne evyll wark doth contayne
Glydeth his wey, thou maft hym not reftrayne :
The evyl then in thy breft cleveth behynde
Wyth grudge of hert and hevynes of mynde.

THE LOSSE OF A BETTER THYNG.

When thou laboreft thy pleafure for to bye
Upon the pryce loke thou the well advyfe,
Thou felleft thy foule therfore evyn by & by
To thy mooft uttre difpiteoufe enemyes :
A mad merchaunt, o folifsh merchaundyfe,
To by a tryfle, o chyldyfshe rekenynge,
And pay therefore fo dere a precyoufe thyng.

THIS LYFE A DREME AND A SHADOW.

This wretched life (the truft & confidence
Of whofe contynuaunce maketh us bolde to fynne)
Thou perceiveft well by experience,
Sith that houre in which hit dyde begynne,
Hit holdeth on the courfe and wyll not lynne,[43]
But faft hit rynneth on and paffen fhall
As doth a dreme or a fhadowe on the wall.

DETH AT OUR HAND AND UNWARE.

Confydre well that ever nyght and daye,
Whyle that we befyly provyde and care
For oure difport revell myrth and play,
For plefaunt melody and deynty fare :
Deth ftelyth on ful flyly, and unware
He lieth at hand and fhall us entreprife
We not[47] how foone nor in what maner wife.

FERE OF IMPENITENT DEPARTYNGE.

If thou fholdeft God offende thynke how therfore
Thou were forthwith in very jeoperdous cafe
For happely thou fholdeft not lyve an houre more
Thy fynne to clenfe, & though thou haddeft fpace.
Yet peradventure fholdeft thou lacke the grace :
Well ought we then be a ferde to done offence
Impenitent left we departen hens.

ETERNALL REWARDE ETERNALL PAYNE.

Thou feeft this worlde is but a thorowfare,
Se thou behave the wifely with thy hooft :
Hens muft thou nedes departe naked & bare,
And after thy deferte loke to what cooft
Thou arte convayed at fuche tyme as thy gooft
From this wretched carkas fhall dyffever :
Be hit joye or payne, endure hit thou fhall for ever.

THE NATURE AND DYGNITE OF MAN.

Remembre how God hath made the refonable
Lyke unto his image and fygure,
And for the fuffred paynes intollerable
That he for aungell never wolde endure.
Regarde o man thyne excellent nature :
Thou that with aungell arte made to bene egall,
For very fhame be not the devylles thrall.

THE PEACE OF A GOOD MYNDE.

Why loveft thou fo this brotle worldes joye :
Take all the myrth, take all the fantafies,
Take every game, take every wanton toye,

Take every fport that man can the devyfe :
And amonge them all on warantyfe
Thou fhalt no pleafure comparable fynde
To th'ynwarde gladnes of a vertuous mynde.

THE GRETE BENEFYCES OF GOD.

By fyde that God the bought & fourmed both
Many a benefyte haft thou receyved of his :
Though thou have moved hym often to be wroth
Yet he the kepte hath and brought us up to this,
And dayly calleth upon the to his blys :
How mayft thou then to hym unlovynge be
That ever hath ben fo lovynge unto the.

THE PAYNFULL CROSSE OF CHRYST.

Whan thou in flame of the temptacyon fryeft
Thynke on the very lamentable payne,
Thynke on the pyteoufe croffe of wofull Chryft,
Thynke on his blode bet out at every vayne,
Thynke on his precyous herte kerved in twayne :
Thynke how for thy redempcyon all was wrought :
Let hym not lefe that he fo dere hath bought.

THE WYTNES OF MARTYRES & EXAMPLE OF SAYNTES.

Synne to withftonde faye not thou lakkeft myght :
Suche allegacyons folye hit is to ufe :
The wytnes of fayntes, & martyrs conftant fyght
Shall the of flouthfull cowardyfe accufe :
God will the helpe yf thou do not refufe :
Yf other have ftande or this thou mayft eft foone :
Nothynge impoffible is that hath bene doone.

66

THE .XII. PROPERTEES OR CONDICYONS OF A LOVER.

To love one alone and contempne all other for yᵗ one.

To thynke hym unhappy that is not with his love.

To adourne hym felfe for the pleafure of his love.

To fuffre all thyng, thoughe hit were deth, to be with his love.

To defyre alfo to fuffre fhame harme for his love, and to thynke that hurte fwete.

To be with his love ever as he may, yf not in dede yet in thought.

To love all thynge yᵗ perteyneth unto his love.

To coveite the prayfe of his love, and not to fuffre ony dyfprayfe.

To beleve of his love all thynges excellent, & to defyre that all folke fholde thynke the fame.

To wepe often with his love : in prefence for joye, in abfence for forowe.

To languyfshe ever and ever to burne in the defyre of his love.

To ferve his love, nothyng thynkynge of ony rewarde or profyte.

THE . XII. PROPERTEES WE HAVE AT LENGTH MORE OPENLY EXPRESSED IN BALADE AS HIT FOLOWETH.⁴⁸

The fyrſt poynt is to love but one alone,
And for that one all other to forfake :
For who fo loveth many loveth none :
The flode that is in many chanelles take
In eche of them fhall feble ſtremes make :

The love that is devyded amonge many
Unneth fuffyfeth that ony parte have ony.

So thou that haft thy love fet unto God
In thy remembraunce this enprynt & grave :
As he in foverayne dignyte is odde,
So wyll he in love no partynge felowes have :
Love hym therfore with all that he the gave :
For body, fowle, wytte, connynge, mynde & thought,
Parte wyll he none, but eyther all or nought.

THE SECONDE PROPERTE.

Of his love lo the fyght and company
To the lover fo glad and pleafaunt is,
That who fo hath the grace to come therby
He judgeth hym in perfyte joye and blys :
And who fo of that company doth myffe,
Lyve he in never fo profperous eftate,
He thynketh hym wretched and infortunate.

So fholde the lover of God efteme that he
Whiche all the pleafure hath, myrth and difporte
That in this worlde is poffible to be,
Yet tyll the tyme that he maye ones reforte
Unto that blyffed joyfull hevenly porte
Where he of God may have the glorious fyght,
Is voyde of parfyte joye and delyght.

THE THYRDE PROPERTE.

The thyrde poynt of a parfyte lover is
To make hym frefshe, to fe that all thynge bene
Apoynted well and nothynge fet a mys,

But all well fafshoned, propre, goodly & clene :
That in his parfone there be nothynge fene
In fpeche, apparayll, gefture, loke or pace
That may offende or mynyfshe ony grace.

So thou that wylte with God gete in to favoure
Garnyfshe thy felfe up in as goodly wyfe,
As comely be, as honeft in behavoure
As hit is poffyble for the to devyfe :
I meane not hereby that thou fholdeft aryfe,
And in the glaffe upon thy body prowle,[49]
But with fayre vertue to adourne thy foule.

THE FOURTH PROPERTE.

If love be ftronge, hote, myghty, and fervent,
There may no trouble, greyfe or forow fall,
But that the lover wolde be well content
All to endure and thynke hit eke to fmall,
Thoughe hit were deth : fo he myght therwithall
The joyfull prefence of that perfone get
On whom he hath his herte and love i set.

Thus fholde of God the lover be content
Ony dyftres or forow to endure,
Rather then to be from God abfent,
And glad to dye, fo that he maye be fure
By his departynge hens for to procure
After this valey darke the hevenly lyght,
And of his love the gloryoufe fight.

THE FYFT PROPERTE.

Not onely a lover content is in his herte,
But coveyteth eke and longeth to fuftayne

Some laboure, incommodite or fmarte,
Loffe, adverfyte, trouble, greyfe or payne :
And of his forowe joyfull is and fayne,
And happy thynketh hymfelfe that he may take
Some myfadventure for his lovers fake.

Thus fholdeft thou that loveft God alfo
In thyne herte wyfshe, coveyte and be glad
For hym to fuffre trouble, payne and woo :
For whom yf thou be never fo woo beftade,
Yet thou ne fhalt fufteyne (be not adrad)
Halfe the dolour, gryefe and adverfyte
The he all redy fuffred hath for the.

THE . VI . PROPERTE.

The parfyte lover longeth for to be
In prefence of his love both nyght & daye :
And yf hit happely fo be fall that he
May not as he wolde : he wyl yet as he may
Ever be with his love, that is to faye,
Where his hevy body nyl be brought [50]
He wyll be converfaunt in mynd and thought.

Lo in lyke maner the lover of God fholde
At the left in fuche wyfe as he may,
If he may not in fuche wyfe as he wolde,
Be prefent with God and converfaunt alway :
For certes who fo lyft he may purvey,
Though al ye worlde wolde hym therfro beryven,
To bere his body in erth, his mynde in heven.

THE .VII . PROPERTE.

There is no page or fervaunt moft or left
That doth upon his love attende & wayte,

There is no lytle worme, no fymple beft,
Ne none fo fmall a tryfle or conceyte,
Lafe, gyrdell, poynt, or propre glove ftrayte :
But that yf to his love hit have ben nere,
The lover hath hit precyous, leyfe, & dere.

So every relyque, image or pyĉture,
That doth pertayne to Goddes magnyfycence,
The lover of God fholde wyth all befy cure
Have hit in love, honoure and reverence :
And fpecyally gyve them preemynence
Which dayly done his bleffed body nyrche,[51]
The quyk relyques, the mynyftres of his chyrch.

THE . VIII . PROPERTE.

A very lover above all erthly thyng
Coveyteth and longeth evermore to here
T'honoure, lawde, commendacyon and prayfyng,
And every thyng that may the fame clere
Of his love : he may in no manere
Endure to here that therefro myghten vary,
Or ony thyng fowne in to the contrary.

The lover of God fholde coveyte in lyke wyfe
To here his honoure, worfhyp, laude and prayfe,
Whofe fovereygne goodnes none herte may compryfe,
Whom hell, erth, and all the heven obayfe :
Whofe parfyte lover ought by no maner wayes
To fuffre the curfed wordes of blafphemy,
Or ony thynge fpoken of God unreverently.

THE . IX . PROPERTE.

A very lover beleveth in his mynde,
On whom fo ever he hath his herte i bent,

That in that perfone men may nothynge fynde
But honorable, worthy and excellent,
And eke furmountynge farre in his entent
All other that he hath knowen by fyght or name :
And wolde that every man fholde thynke the fame.

Of God lyke wyfe fo wonderfull and hye
All thynge efteme & judge his lover ought,
So reverence, worfhyp, honour & magnyfye,
That all the creatures in this worlde i wrought
In comparyfon fholde hee fet at nought :
And glad be yf he myght the meane devyfe
That all the worlde wolde thynken in lyke wyfe.

THE . X . PROPERTE.

The lover is of colour deed and pale :
There wyll no flepe in to his eyen ftalk :
He favoreth neyther mete, wyne, nor ale :
He myndeth not what men about hym talke :
But ete he, drynke he, syt, lye downe or walke,
He burneth ever as hit were with a fyre
In the fervent hete of his defyre.

Here fholde the lover of God enfample take
To have hym contynually in remembraunce,
With hym in prayer and medytacyon wake,
Whyle other playe, revell, fynge, and daunce :
None erthly joy, difport or vayne plefaunce
Solde hym delyte, or ony thynge remove
His ardent mynde from God his hevynly love.

72

THE . XI . PROPERTE.

Dyverfly paffyoned is the lovers herte :
Now plefaunt hope, now drede and grevous fere,
Now parfyte blyffe, now bytter forowe fmarte :
And whether his love be with hym or elles where,
Oft from his eyen there falleth many a tere :
For very joy when they togyther be :
Whan they be fondred for adverfyte.

Lyke affeccyons feleth eke the breft
Of Goddes lover in prayer and meditacyon :
Whan that his love lyketh in hym reft
With inwarde gladnes of pleafaunt contemplacyon,
Out breke the teres for joye and delectacyon :
And whan his love lyft efte to parte hym-fro,
Out breke the teres agayne for payne & woo.

THE .XII. · PROPERTE.

A very lover wyll his love obaye :
His joye it is and all his appetyght
To payne hym felfe in all that ever he maye,
That parfone in whom he fet hathe his delyght
Dylygent to ferve bothe day and nyght
For very love without ony regarde
To ony profyte, gwerdon or rewarde.

So thou lyke wyfe that haft thyne herte i fet
Upwarde to God : fo well thy felfe endevere,
So ftudyoufly that nothynge may the let
Nor fro his fervyce ony wyfe diffevere :
Frely loke eke thou ferve that therto never

Truſt of rewarde or profyte do the bynde,
But onely faythfull herte & lovynge mynde.

Wageles to ſerve .iii. thynges may us move :
Fyrſt yf the ſervyce ſelfe be deſyrable :
Seconde yf they whom that we ſerve & love
Be very good and very amyable :
Thyrdely of reaſon be we ſervyſable
Without the gapynge after ony more
To ſuche as have done moche for us before.

Serve God for love then, not for hope of mede.
What ſervyce maye ſo deſyrable be
As where all turneth to thyne owne ſpede.
Who is ſo good, ſo lovely eke as he,
Who hath all redy done ſo moche for the,
As he that fyrſt the made, and on the rode
Eft the redemed with his precyous blode.

A PRAYER OF PICUS MIRANDULA UNTO GOD.

O holy God of dredefull mageſtee
Verely one in .iii . and thre in one :
Whom aungelles ſerve, whoſe werk all creatures be,
Which heven and erth directeſt all alone :
We The beſeche good Lorde with wofull mone,
Spare us wretches & waſshe away our gylt
That we be not by thy juſt angre ſpylt.

In ſtraye balance of rygorous judgement
If Thou ſholdeſt our ſynne pondre and wey :
Who able were to bere thy punyſshment.

The hole engyne of all this worlde I faye,
The engyne that enduren fhall for aye,
With fuche examynacyon myght not ftande
Space of a moment in thyne angry hande.

Who is not born in fynne originall.
Who doth not actuall fynne in fondry wyfe.
But thou good Lorde arte he that fpareft all
With pyteoufe mercy temperynge juftyce :
For as Thou doeft rewardes us devyce
Above our meryte, fo doeft thou difpence
Thy punyfshement farre undre our offence.

More is thy mercy farre then all our fynne :
To gyve them alfo that unworthy be
More godly is, and more mercy therin.
Howbehit worthy inough are they perdee :
Be they never fo unworthy : whom that he
Lyft to accept : where fo ever he taketh
Whom he unworthy fyndeth worthy maketh.

Wherfore good Lorde that aye mercyfull arte,
Unto thy grace and foverayne dygnyte
We fely wretches crye with humble herte :
Oure fynnes forget and our malygnite :
With pyteous eyes of thy benygnyte
Frendly loke on us ones thyne owne,
Servauntes or fynners whether hit lyketh The.

Synners, yf Thou our cryme beholde, certayne :
Our cryme the warke of our uncorteyfe mynde :
But yf thy gyftes Thou beholde agayne,
Thy gyftes noble wonderfull and kynde :

Thou fhalte us then the fame perfones fynde
Which are to The, and have be longe fpace
Servauntes by nature, chyldren by thy grace.

But this thy goodnes wryngeth us alas :
For we whom grace had made thy chyldren dere
Are made thy gylty folke by our trefpace :
Synne hath us gylty made this many a yere.
But let thy grace, thy grace that hath no pere,
Of our offence furmounten all the peace,[52]
That in our fynne thyne honour may encreace.

For though thy wifdom, though thy foverayn powre
May other wyfe appere fuffycyently :
As thynges whiche thy creatures every houre
All with one voice declare and teftyfye :
Thy goodnes yet, thy fynguler mercy,
Thy pyteous herte, thy gracyous indulgence
Nothynge fo clerely fheweth as our offence.

What but our fynne hath fhewed that mighty love :
Whiche able was thy dredful mageftee
To drawe downe in to erth fro heven above
And crucyfye God : that we poor wretches we
Sholde from our fylthy fynne iclenfed be
With blode and water of thyne owne fyde,
That ftremed from thy blyffed woundes wyde.

Thy love and pyte thus o hevenly Kynge
Our evyll maketh mater of thy goodnes.
O love, o pyte, our welth ay provydynge,
O goodnes fervyng thy fervauntes in diftres.
O love, o pyte, well nygh now thankles.

76

O goodnes, myghty, gracyous and wyfe,
And yet almoft now vanquyfshed with our vyce.

Graunt I The praye fuche hete into myne herte
That to this love of thyne may be egall.
Graunt me fro Sathanas fervyce to aftert,
With whom me rueth fo longe to be thrall.
Graunt me good Lorde and Creatour of all
The flame to quenche of all fynfull defyre,
And in thy love fet all myne herte a fyre.

That whan the journay of this deedly lyfe
My fely gooft hath fynyfshed, and thenfe
Departen muft without his flefshly wyfe,
Alone in to his Lordes hygh prefence :
He may The fynde : o Well of Indulgence :
In thy lordefhyp not as a lorde : but rather
As a very tendre lovynge father.
                    Amen.

Enprynted at London in the Fleteftrete
at the fygne of the Sonne, by me
Wynkyn de Worde.

NOTES.

NOTES.

COLLATION OF MORE'S TEXT
with the original showed that in a few
instances he had inaccurately or inade-
quately rendered it.   In such cases, or
where for any other reason it seemed
desirable, the words of the original are
given in the notes, the letters G. F. P. or P. subjoined in
brackets indicating that the reference is to the Latin life
by Giovanni Francesco Pico or to Pico's works.   A
few misprints have been silently corrected.

1. This lady may be either Jocosa or Joyce, daughter
of Richard Culpeper of Hollingborne, Kent, and wife of
Ralph Leigh, undersheriff of London, or her daughter,
Jocosa or Joyce Leigh, sister of Sir John Leigh who suc-
ceeded to the manor of Stockwell, Surrey, on the death
of his uncle, Sir John Leigh, 27 Aug., 1523.   Tanswell,
"History and Antiquities of Lambeth," pp.   41-2.
Manning and Bray, " History of Surrey," iii. 497-8.

2. Pico was the third son and youngest child of Giovanni Francesco Pico, Count of Mirandola and Concordia
in the Modenese.   He had two brothers, Galeotto, and
Antonio Maria, and three sisters, Catterina, Lucrezia and

81   M

Giulia.   Galeotto had to wife Bianca, daughter of Niccolò d'Este, lord of Ferrara; Antonio Maria married twice, viz., (1) Costanza, daughter of Sante Bentivoglio, lord of Bologna, (2) a Neapolitan lady.   Pico's eldest sister, Catterina, married (1) Leonello Pio, lord of Carpi, by whom she had Alberto, mentioned in connection with Pico's death; (2) Rodolfo, lord of Gonzaga.   Carpi and Gonzaga are little towns in the Modenese.   Lucrezia also married twice, viz. (1) Pino Ordelaffo, lord of Forli; (2) Gherardo Appiani di Piombino, Count of Montagnana.   The third sister, Giulia, took the veil.

Pico's pedigree has been carried back as far as Manfredo of Reggio, a contemporary of Charlemagne; but the descent from the nephew of Constantine is mythical.

"Memorie Storiche della Mirandola," Litta, "Celebr. Fam. Ital." Pico, *Opera* (ed. 1601), *Life* by G. F. Pico; and "Adversus Astrologos," ii. cap. ix.

3. The Boiardi.   Giulia was the daughter of Feltrino Boiardo, first Count of Scandiano, and aunt of the poet, Matteo Maria Boiardo, author of the "Orlando Innamorato." Litta, "Celebr. Fam. Ital." Venturi, "Storia di Scandiano," p. 83.

4. Paulinus was secretary to S. Ambrose, and wrote his life; from which the story in the text is taken.

5. "Flavo et inaffectato capillitio" (G. F. P.).   Apparently Pico was somewhat careless about the arrangement of his hair.

6. Apollonius of Tyana, fl. 70 A.D., travelled throughout the ancient world expounding Neo-Pythagoreanism, and working wonders, esteemed miraculous.

7. For an account of these spurious compositions, written at various dates between the first century before and the third century after Christ, but which were uni-

versally regarded as genuine in Pico's day, see Zeller, " Philosophie der Griechen."

8. Aquinas.

9. With whom Pico was connected by affinity. See note 2.

10. For this vaunt of Epicurus see Diogenes Laertius, "Vitæ Philosph." x. 13 sc. τοῦτον Ἀπολλόδωρος ἐν χρονικοῖς Λυσιφάνους ἀκοῦσαί φησι καὶ Πραξιφάνους· αὐτὸς δὲ οὔ φησιν ἀλλ᾽ ἑαυτοῦ, ἐν τῇ πρὸς Εὐρύδικον ἐπιστολῇ.

11. Pico's conduct in this matter was not altogether so generous as it appears in the text. Soon after his father's death his brothers had fallen out about the partition of the family estates, and matters went so far that in 1473 Galeotto surprised Antonio Maria and incarcerated him in the citadel of Mirandola, while he made himself master of the entire inheritance, apparently ignoring Pico's title altogether. Antonio Maria remained a close prisoner in Mirandola for about two years, at the close of which he was released in deference to the intercessions, or perhaps menaces, of his friends, fled to Rome, and appealed to the Pope. He returned in 1483 with a small army furnished by the Duke of Calabria, possessed himself of Concordia, and negotiated a treaty of partition with his brother. The treaty was, however, by no means strictly observed. Pico had taken no part in the quarrel, and was probably the more ready to cede his rights to his nephew that any attempt to vindicate them for himself would certainly have excited the determined hostility of his brothers. The conveyance was executed on 22 April 1491. " Memorie Storiche della Mirandola," i. 108 ; ii. 43. Calori Cesis, " Giovanni Pico."

12. Girolamo Benivieni, author of the "Canzone dell'

Amore Celeste e Divino" on which Pico wrote the commentary referred to in the Introduction p. 24. For an account of him see Mazzucchelli, "Scrittori Italiani."

13. St. Jerome, author of the Vulgate version of the Bible. The passage referred to is as follows :—"Scimus plerosque dedisse eleemosynam, sed de proprio corpore nihil dedisse ; porrexisse egentibus manum, sed carnis voluptate superatos dealbasse ea quae foris erant, et intus plenos fuisse ossibus mortuorum." " Epistola ad Eustochium Virginem," *Opera* (fol.) i. 65. g.

14. "Potissimum" (G. F. P.), especially. So in " Romaunt of the Rose," l. 1,358-9, the pomegranate is described as a fruyt fulle well to lyke, "*Namely*, to folk whanne they ben sike."

15. A reminiscence of the " De Sapientis Constantia."

16. "Passim " (G. F. P.), on all hands. In fourteenth and fifteenth century literature "by and by" frequently means severally, or one by one, as in " Romaunt of the Rose," l. 4,582, " These were his wordis by and by." The " Promptorum Parvulorum " (Camden Soc.) translates it "sigillatim." Thence the transition to the sense of the text is not difficult.

17. See Introduction, p. xxiii.

18. "Quam primum " (G. F. P.), as soon as possible.

19. See note 6.

20. A reminiscence of Epode II.

21. After leaving Bologna, Pico spent two years at Padua, the stronghold of scholasticism in Italy. He also studied for a time at Ferrara, under Battista Guarino, the humanist, whom in one of his letters he addresses as *præceptor meus*. In 1482 he returned to Mirandola, in the vicinity of which he built himself a little villa, which

he describes as "pleasant enough, considering the nature of the place and district," and on which he wrote a poem now lost. Here he entertained Aldo Manuzio, who about the same time, doubtless by Pico's recommendation, was appointed tutor to his nephew, Alberto Pio, and a Greek scholar, Emanuel Adramyttenus, a refugee from Crete, where the Moslem was triumphant. He now began to correspond with Politian, and on a visit to Reggio made the acquaintance of Savonarola, who had come thither to attend a chapter of Dominicans. In 1483 he went to Pavia, taking with him Emanuel Adramyttenus, who acted as his Greek master. There Emanuel died, and Pico then joined Aldo Manuzio at Carpi. About this time he began the study of the oriental languages, his master being one Jocana, otherwise unknown. In 1484, if not earlier, he went to Florence, and made himself known to Marsilio Ficino, who had then just completed his translation of Plato. Pico urged him to crown his labours by performing the same office for Plotinus. Ficino, who was so little above the common superstitions of his time that he believed firmly in astrology, saw in Pico's unexpected appearance at this critical juncture an event not to be explained by natural causes, and taking his suggestion as a divine monition, forthwith set about the work : nor, when it was completed, did he omit to recount, in dedicating it to Lorenzo, the incident which led to its initiation. Pico appears to have remained at Florence until the latter part of 1485, when we lose sight of him for a time. We obtain, however, a transient glimpse of him in a somewhat novel light from a letter from his sister-in-law, Costanza, to Fra Girolamo, of Piacenza, dated 16 May, 1486, and printed in "Memorie Storiche della Mirandola," ii. 167. From this it appears that he had then recently left Arezzo with a Florentine married lady, who, Costanza is careful to state, "accompanied him voluntarily," but had been attacked by some boors, who cut to pieces his attendants, wounded him in two places, and carried him back to Arezzo. Whether the outrage is imputable to the jealousy of the lady's husband, Costanza cannot say. How the affair ended does not appear, but in the following October we find Pico at Perugia, and in November at Fratta in the Ferrarese. Then followed the visit to Rome, the affair of the Theses, and the journey to France, where he was presented to Charles VIII. After his recall to Italy he resided either at Fiesole or Florence until the summer of 1491, when he accompanied Politian to Venice. They returned to Florence in time to be present at the deathbed of Lorenzo (8 Ap. 1492). The rest of his life Pico spent partly at Ferrara and partly at Florence.

The foregoing brief record of Pico's wanderings reposes mainly upon the evidence afforded by his letters and those of Aldo Manuzio, Politian, and Ficino. Many of these, however, are undated, and all are singularly poor in personal detail. See also Calori Cesis, "Giovanni Pico della Mirandola," 2nd ed., 1872 ; Parr Greswell, "Memoirs of Angelus Politianus," &c.; and Villari's "Savonarola," Eng. tr. 1889, ii. 74.

22. "Insidiosissima correptus est febre" (G. F. P.), "Axes" is of course merely *access*.

23. See Note 2.

24. "Cæli reginam ad se nocte adventasse miro fragrantem odore, membraque omnia febre illa *contusa contractaque* refovisse" (G. F. P.). "Brosed" = bruised ("contusa"). "Frushed" appears to be derived from the

86

French *froisser*, which may mean either to bruise or to rumple ; whence also probably "froyse" used locally for a pancake. See "Promptorium Parvulorum" (Camden Soc.) *Froyse*.

25. See note 2.

26. Charles VIII., to whom Pico had recently been presented. See note 21.

27. Girolamo Savonarola. For what little is known of his relations with Pico see note 21, and his life by Villari, Eng. tr. (1889).

28. "Verum divinis beneficiis male gratus, vel ab sensibus vocatus, detractabat labores (delicatæ quippe temperaturæ fuerat) ; vel arbitratus eius opera religionem indigere, differebat ad tempus : hoc tamen non ut verum sed ut a me conjectatum et præsumptum dixerim" (G. F. P.). But unmindful of God's favours to him, or led away by the senses, he shrank from the labours (he was of a delicate constitution) ; or thinking that religion had need of his services he yet deferred them for a time : not, however, that I state this as truth, but only as what I conjecture or presume to be so.

29. "A diaboli laqueis" (P.), from the snares of the devil. So in Holinshed, "History of Scotland," Ethodius, 194 H. B., we read of "nets and grens" for snaring hares.

30. "Suggeret tibi cum Spiritus qui interpellat pro nobis, tum ipsa necessitas singulis horis quod petas a Deo tuo : suggeret et sacra lectio, quam ut omissis jam fabulis nugisque poetarum semper habeas in manibus etiam atque etiam rogo" (P.). It shall be taught thee both by the Spirit which intercedes for us and by thine own needs every hour what thou shouldest ask of thy God ; and also by the reading of the holy scriptures, which, laying now

87

aside the frivolous fables of the poets, I earnestly entreat thee to have ever in thy hands.

31. The letter is dated from Ferrara, 15 May, 1492, *i.e.* shortly after the death of Lorenzo.

32. A fragment of the lost Neoptolemus of Ennius :—

"Philosophari est mihi necesse, at paucis, nam omnino haut placet;
Degustandum ex ea, non in eam ingurgitandum censeo."

Ribbeck, " Frag. Lat. Reliq." i. 53 ; cf. Cic. " Tusc. Dispt." ii. 1.

33. Epist I. i. *ad fin :—*

"Ad summam : sapiens uno minor est Jove, dives,
Liber, honoratus, pulcher, rex denique regum ;
Præcipue sanus, nisi cum pituita molesta est."

34. " Uti mannus " (P.), like a draught-horse. Doubt-less in More's edition the word was spelt mānus ; hence the curious mistranslation.

35. "*Perusiæ* xv. Octo Mcccclxxx*vi.* anno gratiæ" (P.). It is not easy to account for the double error into which More has here fallen.

36. " Mentientes *propter* eum " (P.), lying (*i.e.* to our disadvantage) because of him.

37. Ps. xxv. 1-5 in the authorized and revised versions. The Vulgate, where it appears as Ps. xxiv., has a slightly different rendering :—"Ad Te Domine levavi animam meam : Deus meus in Te confido, non erubescam : Neque irrideant me inimici mei : etenim universi,qui sustineant Te, non confundentur. Dirige me in veritate tua, et doce me, quia Tu es Deus Salvator meus, et Te sustinui tota die."

38. Ps. xvi. in the authorized and revised versions, xv. in the Vulgate, which is as follows :—"Conserva me Domine, quoniam speravi in Te. Dixi Domino : Deus

meus es Tu, quoniam bonorum meorum non eges. Sanctis qui sunt in terra ejus mirificavit omnes voluntates meas in eis. Multiplicatæ sunt infirmitates eorum : postea acceleraverunt. Non congregabo conventicula eorum de sanguinibus : nec memor ero nominum eorum per labia mea. Dominus pars hereditatis meæ, et calicis mei. Tu es qui restitues hereditatem meam mihi. Funes ceciderunt mihi in præclaris : etenim hereditas mea præclara est mihi. Benedicam Dominum, qui tribuit mihi intellectum : insuper et usque ad noctem increpuerunt me renes mei. Providebam Dominum in conspectu meo semper : quoniam a dextris est mihi ne commovear. Propter hoc lætatum est cor meum, et exultavit lingua mea : insuper et caro mea requiescet in spe. Quoniam non derelinques animam meam in inferno : nec dabis sanctum tuum videre corruptionem. Notas mihi fecisti vias vitæ, adimplebis me lætitia cum vultu tuo : delectationes in dextera tua usque in finem."

39. " By-and-by " is here evidently *forthwith*, and " medyatly " *immediately*.

40. These rules, of which More's verses are rather a paraphrase than a translation, were written by Pico in prose, and were translated into prose by Sir Thomas Elyot, author of the " Boke of the Governour," as follows :

" THE RULES OF A CHRISTIAN LYFE MADE BY JOHAN PICUS THE ELDER ERLE OF MIRANDULA.

" Firſt if to man or woman the way of vertue dothe ſeme harde or paynefull, bycauſe we muſte nedes fyghte agaynſte the fleſhe, the divell, and the worlde, lette hym or her calle to remembraunce, that what fo ever lyfe they wyll chofe accordynge to the worlde, many adverfities, incommodities, moche hevynes and labour are to be fuffred.

" Moreover lette them have in remembraunce, that in welth and worldly poffeffions is moche and longe contention, laborioufe alfo, and ther with unfrutefulle, wherin travayle is the conclufyon or ende of labour, and fynally payne everlaftynge, if thofe thynges be not well ordered and charitably difpofed.

" Remembre alfo, that it is very folifhnes to thinke to come unto heven by any other meane than by the fayde batayle, confidering that our hed and mayfter Chrifte did not afcende unto heven but by his paffion : And the fervaunte oughte not to be in better aftate or condicion than his mayfter or foverayne.

" Furthermore confyder, that this bataile ought not to be grudged at, but to be defired and wifhed for, all though thereof no price or rewarde mought enfue or happen, but onely that therby we mought be conformed or joyned to Chrifte our God and mayfter. Wherefore as often as in refiftinge any temptacion thou dooeft withftande any of the fences or wittes, thinke unto what part of Chriftes paffion thou mayfte applye thy felfe or make thy felfe lyke : As refiftinge glotony, whiles thou doeft punyfhe thy taft or appetite : remembre that Chrifte receyved in his drynke ayfelle myxte with the gall of a beafte, a drinke mofte unfavery and loathfome. Whan thou withdrawefte thy hande from unlefull takinge or kepinge of any thinge, whiche liketh thyne appetite: remembre Chriftes handis as they were faft nayled unto the tree of the croffe. And refifting of pryde, thinke on him, who being very God almighty, for thy fake received the forme

90

of a ſubjecte, and humbled hym ſelfe unto the mooſte vile and reproachefull deathe of the croſſe.

"And whan thou art tempted with wrathe: remembre that He whiche was God, and of all men the moſt juſte or rightwyſe, whan He behelde hym ſelfe mocked, ſpit on, ſcourged, and puniſhed with alle diſpites and rebukes, and ſette on the croſſe amonge errant theves, as if He Hym Selfe were a falſe harlot, He notwithſtanding ſhewed never token of indignacion or that He were greved, but ſuffering al thinges with wonderful pacience, aunſwered al men moſt gentilly. In this wiſe if thou peruſe al thinges one after an other, thou mayſt finde, that there is no paſſion or trouble, that ſhall not make the in ſome parte conformable or like unto Chriſte.

"Alſo putte not thy truſte in mannes helpe, but in the onelye vertue of Chriſte Jeſu, whiche ſayde: Truſte well, for I have vaynquiſhid the worlde. And in an other place He ſayde: The prince of this worlde is caſte oute thereof. Wherfore let us truſte by his onelye vertue, to vaynquiſhe the worlde, and to ſubdue the divell. And therfore oughte we to aſke his helpe by the prayers of us and of his ſainctes.

"Remembre alſo, that as ſoone as thou haſt vanquiſhed one temtation, alway an other is to be loked for: The divell goeth alwaye aboute and ſeketh for hym whome he wolde devoure. Wherfore we ought to ſerve dylygently and be ever in feare, and to ſay with the prophete: I will ſtande alwaye at my defence.

"Take heed more over, that not onelye thou be not vaynquiſhed of the dyvel, that temptith the, but alſo that thou vanquiſhe and overcome him. And that is not onlye whan thou doeſte no ſyn, but alſo whan of that thinge wherin he tempted the, thou takeſt occaſion for to do good.

As if he offrith to the fome good acte to be done to the intent that therby thou mayfte fall into vayneglory : furth with thou thinkinge it not to be thy deede or warke, but the benefitte or rewarde of God, humble thou thy felfe, and judge the to be unkynde unto God in respecte of his manyfolde benefytes.

" As often as thou doeft fyghte, fyght as in hope to van-quifhe, & to have atte the lafte perpetualle peace. For that paradventure God of his abundante grace fhal gyve unto the, and the divell beynge confufid of thy victory, fhall retorne no more agayne. But yet whan thou hafte vayn-quifhid, beare thy felfe fo as if thou fholdeft fighte agayne fhortly. Thus alway in battayle thou mufte thinke on victory : and after victory thou muft prepare the to bataile immediately.

" All though thou feleft thy felfe wil armed and redy, yet flee notwethstandynge all occafyons to fynne. For as the wife man faith : who loveth perylle fhall therein peryfhe.

" In all temptations refyfte the begynnynge, and beate the children of Babilon againe the Stone, which Stone is Chrifte, and the chyldren be yvell thoughtes and imagi-nations. For in longe contynuinge of fynne, feldome warketh medycyne or remedy.

" Remembre, that althoughe in the fayde conflicte of temptation the battayle feemeth to be verye daungeroufe : yet confyder howe moche fweter it is to vanquifhe temp-tation, than to folowe finne, wherto fhe inclyneth the, wherof the ende is repentance. And herein many be foule deceyved, whiche compare not the fwetneffe of victory to the fwetneffe of fynne, but onely compareth battayle to plea-fure. Not withftandyng a man or woman, whiche hathe a thoufande times knowen what it is to gyve place to tempta-tion, fhoulde ones affaye, what it is to vanquifhe temptation.

" If thou be tempted, thynke thou not therfore that God hathe forfaken the, or that he fetteth but lyttell by the, or that thou art not in the fight of God good or per-fecte : but remembre, that after Sayncte Paule hadde feene God, as He was in his divinitie, and fuche fecrete mifteryes as be not lefull for any man to fpeake or reherce, he for all that fuffred temptation of the flefhe, wherwith God fuffred hym to be tempted, left he fhoulde be affaulted with pryde. Wherin a man ought to confider that Saynt Paule, which was the pure veffell of election, and rapte in to the thyrde heven, was not withftandynge in perylle to be proude of his vertues, as he faith of hym felfe. Wherfore above al temptations manne or woman oughte to arme theym moofte ftronglye agaynfte the temptation of pryde, fens pryde is the rote of all myfchyfe, agaynfte the whiche the onelye remedye is to thynke alway that God humbled hym felfe for us unto the croffe. And more over that deth hath fo humbled us whether we wyl or no, that our bodyes fhal be the meate of wormes lothefome and venymoufe."

41. "Recordare illum felle potatum et aceto"(P.). For " eysell " cf. Shakespeare, Hamlet, v. i. l. 264, "Woo't drink up eisel?" and Sonnet, cxi. l. 10, " Potions of eisel 'gainst my strong infection."

42. "Wood" or *wode* in the sense of *mad* is not uncommon in our older writers. So Demetrius in " A Midsummer Night's Dream," ii. 1, l. 192,

> " And here am I, and wode within this wood,
> Because I cannot find my Hermia."

43. " Preace " would seem to be a corruption of *prest*, ready, used substantivally, " put thyself in preace " mean-

ing *make thyself ready*.   See Skeat, " Etymological
Dictionary of the English Language," art. *Press*.

44. Cf. Ps. cxxxvii. 8, 9: " O daughter of Babylon,
who art to be destroyed; happy shall he be, that rewardeth
thee as thou hast served us.   Happy shall he be, that
taketh and dasheth thy little ones against the stones."

45. Here More speaks in *propria persona*, with perhaps
a *double entendre* in the " We More."   There is nothing
in Pico corresponding to the verses which follow.

46. For "lynne," cease, cf. Spenser, " Faery Queen," i.
canto v. 35.

> " And Sisiphus an huge round stone did reele
> Against an hill, ne might from labour lin."

47. "Not" is for *ne wot*, *i.e.* know not.   So Chaucer
concludes the description of the Merchant in the Prologue
to the " Canterbury Tales," l. 286 :

> " But soth to sayn I n'ot how men him call." ·

48. The stanzas on the " Propertees " are original
except the last two, which are a paraphrase of the following sentence :—

" Solemns autem ad hoc induci præcipue ex tribus
causis.   Prima est quando servitium ipsum per se est
appetibile : secunda quando ille cui servimus est in se
valde bonus et amabilis : sicut solemus dicere, servimus
illi propter suas virtutes. Tertia est quando ille prius quam
inciperes multa tibi beneficia contulit.   Et hæc tria sunt
in Deo : quia pro servitio ejus nihil naviter accipitur quod
non sit nobis bonum : et quoad animam et quoad corpus :
quia servire ei non est aliud quam tendere ad eum : hoc
est ad summum bonum.   Similiter ipse est optimus et
pulcherrimus et sapientissimus : et habet omnes condi-
tiones quæ solent nos movere ad amandum aliquem et
serviendum ei gratis : et in nos contulit summa beneficia

94

cum nos et ex nihilo creaverit et per sanguinem Filii ab inferno redemerit." (P.) There are, moreover, three principal considerations by which we are accustomed to be impelled to this service. The first is that the service itself is desirable for its own sake. The second arises when he whom we serve is in himself very good and amiable, and we serve him, as we are in the habit of saying, on account of his virtues. The third, when before the commencement of your service he whom you serve has conferred on you many favours. And these three considerations coexist in the case of God, for nothing whatever is accepted by way of His service which is not for our good both of soul and of body : for to serve Him is nothing else but to seek after Him : *i.e.* after the chief good. Likewise He Himself is of all beings the best, and most lovely and wisest : and has in Himself all the properties which are wont to move us to love and serve any one without reward : and has conferred on us the greatest favours, since He has both created us from nothing, and redeemed us from hell by the blood of His Son."

48. Cf. "Promptorium Parvulorum" (Camd. Soc.). " Prollynge, or sekynge. Perscrutatio, investigatio, scrutinum :" and Chaucer, " Canterbury Tales," l. 16880. " Though ye prolle ay, ye shal it never find."

50. Cf. note 47.

51. "Nyrche" has been substituted by way of conjectural emendation for "*wyrche*," which is unintelligible. "Nyrche" as = nourish gives the sort of sense required by the context ; and the eccentric spelling may be merely due to the roughness with which the r was pronounced in More's time.

52. "Peace," cup : from the low Latin, *pecia*. See " Promptorium Parvulorum" (Camden Soc.) *Pece* ; and Du Cange, *Pecia*.

CHISWICK PRESS:—C. WHITTINGHAM AND CO.,
TOOKS COURT, CHANCERY LANE.

www.ingramcontent.com/pod-product-compliance
Lightning Source LLC
Chambersburg PA
CBHW020407030726
47496CB00007B/2342